SACRED VOW

TERRI ANNE BROWNING

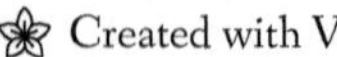 Created with Vellum

The sound of something crashing outside jolted me awake. As I rushed to sit upright, it took me a few moments to realize where I was. The light in the storage room was on, showing me the shelves of supplies the Ink Shoppe kept on hand for all the tattoos Maverick and his father did every day.

"What?" Maverick groaned, his huge hand touching my naked back before he sat up beside me. His touch calmed me somewhat, but the adrenaline of being so forcefully awoken made me tremble. "What's wrong, babe?"

Heart still pounding, I shifted my eyes around the room while I strained to hear the noise that had pulled me so abruptly from sleep. When the only sound I heard was our breathing, I started to relax, and the trembling thankfully began to subside.

"River?" Maverick cupped the back of my head, turning me to look at him. We'd both fallen asleep after having sex once the Ink Shoppe closed. I'd been so blissed out after countless orgasms that I hadn't been able to fight it when my eyes grew heavy, and I'd passed out on the makeshift bed of blankets we kept hidden in the storage room.

"I'm okay," I told him with a tight smile. "It must have been the wind blowing against the trash cans out back."

His eyes narrowed on me. "You've been jumpy all day, baby. Are you sure you're feeling okay?"

Wrapping my arms around his middle, I pressed my face into his wide chest. I was anything but okay, but I couldn't tell him. Normally, I would have told him anything that was on my mind, but it was just better for everyone if I kept this to myself.

At least for now.

My birthday was a few weeks away. Then, I could tell him.

And pray no one tried to kill him once our fathers found out.

Until then, I wouldn't put that kind of stress on him.

The alarm I'd set for myself went off, making me jump at the sudden noise as if a foghorn had blasted right in my ear. Groaning, I kissed Maverick quickly and then pushed to my feet, pulling on my clothes in a rush. I had a midnight curfew, but it was Saturday. My parents never got home from the bar earlier than two—later than that if it was Dad's turn to close—but an urgency was shouting in the back of my head to *hurry, hurry, hurry.*

"Slow down," Maverick said as he took his time standing and pulling on his jeans. "You have plenty of time."

"No," I muttered, lifting my hair out from under my shirt once it was in place. "I need to get home. Something feels...off."

"Hey," he grumbled when I grabbed my purse and

phone. His arms came around me from behind before he turned me to face him. With a finger under my chin, he tipped my head up so I had to meet his gray eyes. Fuck, I loved those eyes. They were so full of love and possessiveness every time they landed on me. Every woman should have a guy look at her the way Maverick looked at me. As if there was no other person in the world they would rather be with for the rest of their life. As if the sun only rose to shine on their love. A lump filled my throat, but I quickly pushed it down. "Tell me what's wrong, River."

Of course he sensed something wrong with me. I would have been surprised if he hadn't. There had always been this connection between us that I hadn't fully understood until I was fourteen. As if we could read each other's minds. I always knew what he was thinking, and more often than not, he knew what was going through my head as well.

Then he'd kissed me one day, and I'd realized why we were so connected.

Maverick Masterson was my soul mate. He was the other half of my heart. The reason I was born was to love him.

But as desperately as I wanted to share what was going on with me right then, I couldn't.

Not yet.

So instead of telling him what was happening I pushed the attention to someone else. "It's...my mom. I think something's up with her." I bit my lip. It wasn't a lie. Mom had been acting weird lately, and I was worried about her. But I'd been so stressed over what was happening to me that I hadn't stopped to really examine what might be going on with her.

Maverick's eyes widened. "What, like she's sick?" He

practically whispered the last word. I understood why. After Aunt Raven had gone through her cancer treatments, we'd all been terrified that something like that could happen to our own mother.

"No," I told him, shaking my head. "I think—" I broke off, not wanting to voice what I really suspected.

"Tell me, Riv," he commanded. "If it's bothering you this badly, I want you to tell me. No secrets, baby."

Tears filled my eyes, because I was keeping a huge secret from him, but it was better—safer—if he didn't know. "I-I think she might be cheating on my dad."

"Fuck," he choked out and pulled my head to his chest. "For real?"

I nodded, taking a moment to get my emotions under control before lifting my head. I did think Mom was cheating on Dad. With the shady way she'd been acting recently, there really wasn't any other explanation. She was sneaking around, hiding things, and lying about places she'd been.

Just a few days before, she'd been late getting home, and when Dad asked her where she'd been, she'd said she was with Aunt Quinn. He hadn't even questioned what I knew was a lie, because I'd been at my aunt and uncle's house. Aunt Quinn had been home all day, but my mother hadn't even stopped by.

So where had she really been?

The thing about my mom was that I knew she loved my dad. She would kill for him. Offer up her own life in exchange for his. But I'd noticed she never fully trusted him. Then again, she'd never seemed to trust any man. I got it, though. Her own father had shot her, had nearly killed her, all because she'd ruined his political career.

If a girl couldn't trust her own daddy, how the fuck was she expected to trust any other male?

But that didn't give her an excuse to cheat on my dad. He was a good man. He took care of Mom and me, working his ass off for the family-owned bar and the MC to provide for us. Not that we needed to worry about money. When Grandpa Hank—the man who'd stepped in as Mom's surrogate father and my honorary grandfather—had passed away, he'd left all his money and other assets to the two of us. Money wasn't an issue. I never had to work if I didn't want to with just the money from the trust fund Grandpa Hank had set up for me when I was born.

Dad was a hard worker, and he'd never once looked at another woman. He loved Mom, worshiped her. All she had to do was bat her lashes at him and he was gone for her, giving her anything she even hinted that she wanted.

And while I knew Mom didn't completely trust Dad, I'd never doubted her love and devotion to him in return.

Not until now.

I honestly didn't want to think she was cheating, but it was the only logical conclusion. Why else would she lie about where she was?

Maverick kissed the top of my head. "It's going to be okay, baby. Don't worry about your parents." His arms tightened around me. "Focus on what you want for your birthday, instead. You still haven't told me what you want."

"Just you," I told him truthfully and tried to burrow myself deeper against him. "I only want you for my birthday."

I felt more than heard his growl as he tipped my head up and lowered his lips to mine. "You will always have me, River."

Wanting nothing more than to melt against him and have him make everything better, I let him hold me for a few more minutes before that overwhelming feeling that I needed to get home began to make me anxious. Pushing up onto my tiptoes, I kissed him hard. "See you tomorrow," I promised before rushing out the back door.

As I hurried to my car, I saw two of the trash cans had been overturned, and one of the bags was ripped open. I didn't give it a second thought, figuring some animal had gotten into it. On the drive home, I had to pass Hannigans', my family's bar, and was thankful to see my dad's bike in its usual spot.

Some of my anxiety eased, but for some reason, I pressed a little harder on the gas. Once I was home and had my car in the garage, I ran inside.

Only to freeze when I walked into the kitchen and found my mother standing at the island with her phone to her ear. Her vehicle hadn't been in the driveway, which had made me think she was still at the bar with Dad. She usually worked there on the weekends because Saturday nights were so crazy when college was in session.

She wasn't dressed as if she'd just come from the bar, though. Nor was she in her pajamas, which was what she normally would have been wearing this late at night if she weren't working.

Mom was wearing a dress that looked like it had been sprayed on her amazing body. It had never been a secret that Kelli Hannigan had once been a stripper at Paradise City before she married my father. She wasn't ashamed of her former profession. She had the kind of body women her age paid good money to achieve. Other than my blond hair and green eyes that I got from Dad, I looked just like her, so

I knew I'd have a body like hers one day if I played my cards right.

"What are you doing home?" I demanded, raking my eyes over her dispassionately. Her hair was styled, and I hadn't seen her wear that much makeup since Mila and Monroe's double wedding back in September. The shoes she was wearing were so high, I knew if I attempted to wear them, I would end up with something broken.

She ended her call without saying goodbye, her eyes narrowing on me as she put her free hand on her hip. "It's after one, River. You should have been home over an hour ago."

"Shouldn't you be at Hannigans' helping Dad?" I sneered, walking farther into the kitchen.

"I had something to take care of," she said with a shrug. Nothing in her face made me think she felt even a little guilty for where she'd been or what she'd been doing dressed the way she was, and that just pissed me off.

"What?" I snipped.

"That's none of your business, little girl," she snapped back. "And just where were you?" Before I could speak, she lifted her hand. "No, don't tell me. I don't want to have to lie to your father about knowing where you were."

I rolled my eyes. "As opposed to lying to him about where *you* were?"

"Your father knew where I was," she told me with a lift of her chin, her eyes daring me to argue with her.

Which I did. "Did he? Yet you lied to him about being with Aunt Quinn two days ago."

Surprise filled her face before she could mask it. "How do you know that?"

I opened the refrigerator and pulled out a bottle of

water. "I was at her house helping Kingston with something. She was home all evening, but I never once saw you, Mother Dear."

When I turned back around to face her, I expected to find her pissed at me. Instead, I found her looking drawn and maybe a little defeated. "If I tell you where I really was, then and tonight, will you promise not to tell your dad about this?"

I slowly took a drink of my water, giving myself time to think about her question. Did I want to know her secret—and add to the one I was already keeping from people I loved?

"Tell me first," I negotiated. "Then I'll decide if it's worth keeping it from Dad."

She pushed her hair back from her face with a heavy sigh. "I've been driving to the surrounding towns, trying to find someone."

Curiosity had me taking a step closer to her. "Who?"

"My niece," she whispered, a quaver in her voice. She cleared her throat, and it was stronger when she spoke again. "You know my father wasn't a good man."

It wasn't a question, but I nodded anyway. A simple internet search could tell anyone who was looking exactly what kind of person my senator grandfather had been. Corrupt didn't even begin to describe the politician. He not only shot Mom, nearly killing her, but he was also responsible for my grandmother's death as well.

"My mother was his mistress," Mom said, her lips pressing into a hard line. This was the first time she'd ever really spoken about her family, so I was listening intently. "I knew there were others, but my mom...she didn't want to believe that. Even though the man was married, she thought she was the only one warming his bed."

"Gross," I muttered.

"A few weeks ago, a social worker contacted me, started asking questions about my father and so on." She squeezed the bridge of her nose, as if she had a bad headache. "A novice could do a search of my maiden name and find out who my parents were. I was the one who exposed Calvin's corruption after all."

"What does this have to do with you cheating on Dad?" I demanded.

Her gaze jerked to mine. "Cheat? On Colt? Are you insane?"

The fury in her voice and on her face made my own anger at her deflate a little. "Are you saying you aren't?"

"I love your father more than anything or anyone—with the exception of you. I would never cheat on him."

Some of the tension straining my muscles began to ease, leaving my entire body feeling a little achy. "Then what have you been doing? You're dressed like that—" I waved my hand at her outfit "—and sneaking around. Where is your car?"

"It broke down on the way home. The stupid onboard computer did an update recently, and I've been having issues ever since. I called Raven. She had it towed to the shop and drove me home." She released a heavy sigh. "She knows everything now too."

"Knows what?" I cried. "Mom, what the hell is going on with you?"

"I was trying to tell you, but you started accusing me of cheating on my husband," she snapped. "So, just be quiet and listen, will you?"

I clamped my lips shut and nodded, motioning for her to go on.

"I got the call from the social worker, asking about my

parents. At first, I didn't know what to think, just figured she was a nosy bitch looking for a story to sell to make a few bucks." She pushed her hair back from her face, and I noticed she looked exhausted. "But when I started telling her to mind her own business, she turned everything upside down."

"How?"

"Turns out, I have a sister I never knew about." She glanced away, her throat working. "Had a sister," she amended. "She died, about eight years ago."

I crossed the kitchen, wrapping my arms around her. Without hesitation, she hugged me back. "I'm so sorry, Mom."

"She was given up for adoption after her mother gave birth to her. Apparently, she'd been underage when she got pregnant. Barely sixteen." Her arms tightened around me. "That bastard had sex with an underage teen. A little girl."

"I'm glad he's dead," I whispered.

"Me too," she agreed.

We were both quiet for a few minutes before she spoke again. "My sister was adopted quickly because she was a baby. She grew up and married a man she met her first year of college. They had a daughter. Delaney." She stroked her hand over my hair lovingly. "But according to the social worker, my sister and her husband were killed in a gas line explosion while on vacation. Delaney was with them, but she survived. Although she did end up with a debilitating injury from the accident."

"What do you mean?" I murmured as gory pictures filled my head. Could my cousin have lost a limb or been disfigured?

"This is all according to the social worker, but from

what she told me, Delaney lost her hearing completely during the explosion. She's been totally deaf ever since."

Sympathy filled me. "But she's alive," I tried to reassure my mom.

"Yeah, honey," Mom agreed, giving me a tight smile that quickly turned into a frown. "The social worker explained that the only living relatives she could find at the time were Delaney's father's sister and her husband. They took her in, but the social worker didn't feel right leaving Delaney there. So, she's been searching for the past eight years in hopes of finding someone else who could take the girl. It was only recently that she found the connection to me and, in desperation, contacted me."

I stood there listening as she told me how Delaney's uncle by marriage was a drug dealer who was suspected to be part of a prostitution ring. The social worker had kept up with Delaney for the past eight years, but she recently had lost contact with her. She was eighteen now, had aged out of the system, but the social worker seemed truly caring and concerned for Delaney.

Mom had met up with the social worker, and the two of them had been trying to find out all they could about the man who was supposed to have been taking care of my cousin all these years.

"Why don't you just tell Dad about all this?" I asked when she told me she'd found out plenty about the drug dealer who was now peddling pussy too, but nothing about her niece.

"Because Colt's technique to get people to talk won't get me the answers I need. He will go in, beat the shit out of a bunch of people, probably put a few bullets in someone, and possibly put Delaney in even more danger than she's already in." Mom shook her head. "I couldn't risk that."

"So, what are you going to do now?"

"After tonight, it's obvious the motherfucker doesn't know anything about Delaney. I think she may have run away." Her face filled with sadness, but there was determination in her eyes when she lifted them to meet mine. "All I can do now is try to find her and pray she's okay."

Pulling my hair up into a ponytail, I frowned down at the schedule in front of me. Uncle Spider had two appointments, but Maverick had four for the evening. Ever since he'd finished his apprenticeship under both his father and then his brother-in-law, Lyric, he'd gotten popular. I booked more appointments for him than I did his dad, but most of them were from college kids.

And eighty percent of those were female.

I knew Mav would never cheat on me, but that didn't stop the whores from trying to tempt him. I hated when he had to ink a girl. They took one look at my man and decided the best place for their new tattoo was on their boobs, rib cage, or along the top of their bikini line.

Just the week before, he'd had to do one on the top of some chick's inner thigh, and I'd had to sit out front and listen to her giggle, telling him he was tickling her.

Afterward, once the stupid skank had left, he'd taken one look at my face and pulled me into the storage room, where he fucked me hard against the wall to show me I was the only one he wanted. But that didn't stop me from getting jealous.

I told myself that once we could be out in the open about our relationship, and I could tell any slutbunny who walked through the door that Maverick Masterson belonged to me, I would calm down. But I knew deep down that even when everyone was finally clued in to the fact that we were together, I was still going to be jealous of every girl who even looked in Mav's direction.

"Hey, River," Uncle Spider greeted as he walked through the front door. He rubbed a hand over his shaved head before combing his fingers through his graying beard. Simply put, the MC enforcer was a silver fox. The man was sexy as hell, and other than the fact that Maverick had his mother's gray eyes, he looked just like his dad. When I saw Uncle Spider, I could picture his son looking just like him when he was the enforcer's age. "Can you reschedule my second appointment, honey? I have to leave early this evening to take care of something."

I gave him a smile, already picking up the phone to do as he requested. "No problem."

I'd been working at the Ink Shoppe since I was fifteen, just answering the phone and booking appointments. It wasn't much, and I hadn't really considered it work since all I did was pick up the phone when it rang. I'd only wanted was to be close to Maverick when he was in the shop or hang out with Mila when she used to work there. But once Mila started running Lyric's place, I'd gone from being given a few twenties every week directly from Uncle Spider's wallet, to getting an actual paycheck. All for doing stuff I didn't mind doing just so I could be close to the man I loved.

It was a sweet gig. The only downside being that I had

to hear those stupid skanks giggle and try to flirt with Maverick during their appointments.

I wouldn't give it up for anything, though. I enjoyed it more than I knew I would working at Hannigans'. Not that my dad would actually let me work at the bar until I was older, but I didn't ever want to work there. It was family-owned, and Dad always said one day I would get his share in it, but I didn't want it. Between Kingston and Jack and my other cousins, I figured the place would be just fine without me. I would give them my share in the place when it came to me, because I planned on helping Mav run the Ink Shoppe just like Mila did with Lyric.

Although, Mila and I had been talking lately about starting up our own business, too. The building right beside Lyric's place was for rent with the option to buy, and Mila had put the idea in my head of the two of us turning it into our own store, exclusively for women. We would sell everything from maternity clothes to intimate items. It was something my friend had been thinking about since she was pregnant.

Creswell Springs was a small town. Everyone had to drive over an hour away just to do some real shopping, which was a pain in the ass. Especially when a woman was pregnant and with few options to stop for a bathroom break on the hour-long drive to the nearest mall. And when that pregnant woman had been pregnant with twins bouncing on her bladder every five seconds, making her have to pee, it made the drive excruciatingly longer.

There were a few small boutiques in town, but none of them that catered to a woman's *every* need.

But Mila didn't want to explore the venture on her own. Between the two of us, we already had good experience running a business. Once I turned eighteen, I would have my trust fund that I could do anything I wanted with. Investing some of it in a place that was partially my own seemed like a hell of an idea to me.

And then I could focus on it instead of hearing some bitch in heat panting over my man who wouldn't give her the time of day.

I quickly rescheduled Uncle Spider's appointment for early the following week and then took care of the short list of things needing my attention before the shop officially opened for the day. Unless Mav or his dad had an early morning appointment, the Ink Shoppe didn't open until five Tuesday through Friday. On Saturdays, we opened at noon and closed at eleven.

There were only a few more weeks left of school, but once it was out, things would slow down a little around the shop. The two men would still have appointments most days, but they wouldn't be booked back-to-back like they were when the local college was in session.

Most days, I was the first one in the shop, unless one of the Masterson men had an earlier appointment. Which meant I had control over the music that was played. Luckily for them, I had good taste in music. But when I was mad at Maverick, I tended to torture him with the easy listening channel.

Grinning to myself, I switched the music over before starting on my homework. Ten minutes later, Maverick walked through the door. I didn't need to look up to know he'd arrived. Some sixth sense always told me when he was in the same room. When his eyes landed on me, my body reacted instantly, and I immediately started craving him.

"Hey, beautiful," he greeted, but I still didn't look up from my work. "Fuck…" he muttered when he heard what was playing through the speaker system. "What did I do?"

I kept my face lowered, pretending to read so he wouldn't see the amusement in my eyes. "What do you mean?"

"You're pissed," he grumbled, his shadow falling over the counter I was sitting at.

"Am I?" I turned the page, finding an answer to the study guide I didn't have time to finish in class earlier. "Did you do something you shouldn't?"

He was quiet for a long moment, and I knew he was trying to remember if he'd done something that could have caused me to be mad at him. "Help me out here, River. I'm coming up with nothing. I haven't done shit since I saw you last night."

"Ah babe, it's cute that you think I don't know exactly what you do every moment you're not with me." I finally lifted my head and winked at him. His eyes brightened at the sight of my smile, and his shoulders relaxed. "I'm just fucking with you, Mav." Picking up the remote, I turned the music back to the usual rock station I kept it on.

He blew out a loud sigh. "Thank fuck," he muttered. "So, we're good?"

"Better than good." I wanted to lean across the counter to kiss him, but Uncle Spider was in his office not thirty feet away, with the door open.

As if he were craving a kiss just as much as I was, Mav shot his gaze over my shoulder. His jaw flexed, but then he gave me that sweet smile of his that only I ever got to be the recipient of. "Just a few more days and then I can kiss you anytime I want," he promised.

A mixture of excitement and trepidation clenched low in my gut. Once my dad knew about Maverick and me, everything would be okay. But him knowing about and actually accepting my relationship were two entirely different things. I wasn't confident that Dad would be very under-standing. I was his little princess, and he'd always said no man would ever be good enough for me in his eyes.

But in my eyes, there was no one better than Maverick.

"Love you," I whispered.

His gray eyes filled with heat. "Love you, baby," he whispered back before forcing himself to step away from the counter. "I have a little work still to do on the first client's art. Let me know when they get here."

"Sure thing, boss," I said with a sassy little smirk that had his nostrils flaring. "Get to work, lazy."

He turned his back on me, but I watched as he pulled his phone from his jeans pocket. As he walked away, a text popped up on my phone.

Mav: *I'll work you later, baby.*

I pressed my legs together, fighting the throb that pulsed at just reading his words.

Me: *Promises. Promises.*

Dropping my phone back on the counter, I forced myself to focus on my schoolwork. Happiness bubbled through my entire body.

Until the door opened and in walked Maverick's first appointment.

Was it wrong to want to scratch up a person's pretty face as soon as you set eyes on them? That was exactly what I wanted to do when the blonde walked through the door in a pair of cutoff shorts that left her ass cheeks hanging out and a top that was little more than a bralette. Her hair was styled in a sexy, disheveled kind of way that made people think she'd just had wild sex. She was wearing designer heels, which told me she was one of the rich college girls from Trinity.

Her skin was ink-free, so I knew this was her first tattoo,

but she didn't look nervous like some first-time clients were. No, there was heat in her eyes instead of anxiety and fear of the unknown.

Jealousy began to burn through me, and my stomach started to churn. Gritting my teeth, I closed my book and stood. "Welcome to the Ink Shoppe. Can I help you?"

Her light-brown eyes slid over me, taking in my loose jeans and the black tank top I was wearing. Between my ponytail and makeup-free face, I probably looked younger than I really was, which, of course, made this girl consider me a non-threat to her.

"I have a date with Maverick," she said as she walked toward the counter, her glossy lips lifting in a snide little smile.

My hands fisted, but she couldn't see them with me standing behind the counter. I wanted nothing more than to shred her pretty face, but I knew that would cause problems all around. "Sure," I muttered. "Give me a moment."

She nodded, and I walked into the back toward Maverick's room. He was sitting at his art station, drawing. His back was to me, and I took a moment to cool my jealousy by watching him. He'd pulled off his cut, and it was hanging on the wall, leaving him in a band T-shirt that stretched tightly across his muscled back. His short dark hair was standing up slightly on top as if he'd carelessly run his fingers through it a few times. What little I could see of his face told me he was deep in thought as he sketched the addition to the tattoo he was creating.

Glancing over my shoulder to make sure Uncle Spider was still in his office, I walked into Maverick's room. Just as I reached him, his arm shot out and snaked around me, pulling me down onto his lap, and he buried his face in my neck. "Fuck, baby, you smell so good."

Shivering as he kissed just under my ear, I arched into his caressing lips. "Your appointment is here," I informed him in a tight voice.

"Yeah? Good for her." He bit down on my shoulder before lifting his head. "Uh oh." He tightened his arms around me. "You really are pissed now."

"She said she has a date with you," I hissed.

His index finger curved under my chin, lifting my head so our gazes locked. "I love you."

"I love you too," I whispered.

"I'm yours, River."

Hearing that helped ease some of my anger and jealousy. "And I'm yours."

He gave me that sweet smile that was mine alone. "Go get your books, and come in here while I'm doing her piece. You'll hear the door if anyone else comes in."

"No, it's okay," I said, shaking my head as I stood. "I trust you."

"I know you do," he assured me. "But I want you in here with me."

I gave him a quick hug. "Okay. Should I tell the skank princess to come back, or do you need more time?"

He grinned. "I'm nearly finished, but I need her approval before I print it."

I sighed, exhaustion suddenly pushing down on me. "Okay, I'll send her back."

"River." I paused at the door when he called my name. "You are my everything."

I glanced at him over my shoulder. "And you're mine."

TWO

MAVERICK

ONE OF THE FIRST THINGS I'D LEARNED WHILE apprenticing under my brother-in-law was not to roll my eyes at the client. My dad hadn't taught me that during the months I'd watched and worked under him. He had no patience for people who didn't take getting ink seriously.

Lyric had been different, though, teaching me things I probably never would have learned without his help. Like how to help some of the more nervous ones keep calm during their first time. And the not-rolling-your-eyes thing was definitely something that had come in handy.

His teachings helped me get the client list I now had, but sometimes it was hard to keep my face from showing how annoyed I was. Especially when my girl was sitting only a few feet away and some chick was trying to flash me her pussy every two minutes.

"Sit the fuck still," I barked, fed up. I doubted even Lyric could have kept his cool long enough to deal with this chick, but then again, my sister probably would have already had a handful of this bitch's hair in one hand as she dragged her out of her husband's shop.

The girl jumped, startled by the sudden menace in my voice. "Okay," she said after a moment of stunned silence before rolling her eyes. "Jeesh, calm down. I'm just trying to get comfortable."

"You have needles digging into your bikini line," River muttered behind me, keeping her gaze focused on her schoolwork. "I doubt there is a comfortable position right now."

The blonde on my table huffed. "Shouldn't you be watching the front or something?"

"She's here because I want her here," I snapped, adding more ink before touching the needle to her skin again. The piece she wanted was small and didn't require a lot of shading, so I was almost done. Thank fuck, because this chick was giving me a raging headache.

As soon as the needle touched her skin, she whined at the discomfort and began to squirm again, causing the protective padding I'd had River place in the top of the chick's shorts to shift, showing me yet another half inch of her skin. Soon, her pussy lips would be exposed, and the thought turned my stomach.

It wasn't the first time a client thought she could try to tempt me by picking a suggestive place for their tattoo and then try to seduce me by showing me her tits or pussy. Even if I didn't have River, I would have been turned off by their efforts. I'd never been tempted by an easy lay, and the clients who tried to get me to fuck them reeked of desperation.

I was nearly finished when the buzzer alerting us to the front door opening grabbed River's attention. She stood to see who had arrived then returned a minute later. "That must be the box that arrived yesterday," she said as she walked past my room.

I glanced up just as Lyric followed her toward the storage room. He had a car seat in one hand, and I saw the top of my nephew's head. At a guess, I figured it was Ian because he was the troublemaker of the twins, and only Lyric and my dad could make him behave. Isaac, on the other hand, was the more even-tempered of the two, always wanting to cuddle with anyone, and basically a momma's boy.

Lyric said Ian was more like his own twin, Luca, while Isaac was one hundred percent his father. Even at just four months old, Ian was already a pain in the ass, but I loved that rotten little beast.

Finally finished with the tattoo, I pushed back from the table the chick was lying on. "Take a look in the mirror before I bandage you up."

While she stood, I turned my back, getting her after-care instructions and samples of the ointment we suggested all our clients use. Lyric had connections, and he'd worked out a deal with the company that made the ointment that was formulated specifically for tattoo aftercare.

"Wow, it's so pretty," the client, whose name I couldn't have remembered even if there were a gun to my head, gushed. "You're really talented."

Ignoring the compliment, I waited until she was back on the table before turning around.

Only to wish I'd waited for River to return before I did. The tiny shorts she was wearing were pulled down to her thighs now, showcasing her bare pussy. "Like what you see?" she purred, stroking her fingers over herself.

I quickly averted my eyes and stood.

"Hey, Dad," I called as I left the room. "Can you patch this chick up for me?"

He met me at the door, a frown on his face. "What's up?"

"She took her fucking pants off," I told him with a shudder. "And now she's touching herself. I'm not into easy."

He grimaced. "I feel ya, son. Wasn't River in there with you?"

"She's getting something for Lyric," I explained, my gaze going to the door to the storage room, where they still were. "If you don't want to patch her up for me, could you at least come in and be my witness?"

I didn't need this chick to get pissed at me and then start saying I touched her or some shit like that. Or worse, screaming I molested or raped her just to get back at me for shooting her down. I'd never had someone do that to me before, but I'd heard too many horror stories not to be cautious.

"Nah, son. I got you covered." He passed me and walked into my room. "Pull your clothes up, girl. I don't have time to be airing out this place because you decided to make it smell like rotten pussy."

A strangled laugh had me looking back at the storage room to find Lyric standing in the doorway. A moment later, River appeared beside him, a box in her hands. "Found it," she said triumphantly. "I don't know how it got all the way in the back like that. I swear I put it..." She trailed off, a frown pulling her brows together as she looked down at the label on the box. "Does this look like blood to you?"

Lyric dropped his gaze to it. "Maybe the delivery guy scratched himself," he suggested. Taking the box from her, he carried it in one hand while holding on to the car seat in the other. "Thanks, River. I need this ink for a back piece I'm doing tonight."

River shook her head, causing her frown to disappear as

she gave my brother-in-law a smile. "No problem. I didn't know it was yours, or I would have brought it to you. Sorry you had to come all the way over here with the baby demon." Crouching down, she kissed Ian's cheek, causing him to giggle. "Be good, little dude."

When she pulled back, I saw my nephew had latched on to River's tank top and was pulling it down, exposing her bra. I couldn't blame the kid. Her tits were perfect. I copped a feel any chance I got, too. Laughing, she untangled his chubby fist and nipped at his fingers, making him giggle again.

Lyric sighed. "I guess he's hungry. I better get him back so Mila can feed him."

"Yeah," she agreed with another one of her sweet laughs. "He's a boob man, just like every other male in the universe." Her green eyes lifted to me, and I winked, causing her to blush prettily.

"Mila wanted me to remind you that she's meeting with the real estate agent tomorrow. Do you want her to pick you up from here and the two of you drive over together?"

"I'll call her later, and we can discuss it," River told him, dropping her gaze back to Ian. "Okay, baby demon. Don't be causing your momma any trouble. Auntie River loves you, little man."

"This is Luca Version 2.0," Lyric grumbled. "Telling him not to cause trouble is the equivalent of giving him permission to burn down the house."

I grinned. "Sounds like you're getting karma for something, brother."

Lyric grunted unhappily. "Apparently, fate got me mixed up with my brother. He's the one who should have a little monster to chase after." But he grinned as he lifted the car seat higher. "That's okay, though. I'm sure when Violet has her baby, he will get all the karma he deserves shoved up his ass. Right, buddy? Uncle Luca is going to be twisted inside out when Vi has her baby girl."

Ian gave a loud squeal that caused us all to laugh just as Dad came out of my room. "What are you screaming about, kid?"

At the sound of his grandpa's voice, Ian started kicking his legs and raised his arms. Dad walked up to Lyric and took the car seat from him, lifting Ian up so they were eye to eye. Spider Masterson was a feared MC enforcer. I'd seen grown men piss themselves when having to face down my dad's wrath. But when he had one of his four grandbabies in his arms, he turned into a big teddy bear.

And there wasn't a single man alive who gave him shit about it either.

My aunts, however, were a different story. They thought it was hilarious that he melted into a puddle of goo for his grandchildren. Meanwhile, my mom couldn't seem to keep her hands off him when he turned into a big softy with Mila's and Monroe's babies. I should think it was gross, but really, I wanted River to have that exact same reaction when we had our own grandbabies to gush over and spoil later in life.

While Dad was cooing down at Ian, my client came out of my room. She didn't even look at me as she left. River smirked as she followed the chick to the front and watched her go. I was expecting another appointment, so I went with my girl, hoping I could cop a feel or two of my own while Dad was distracted.

Walking up behind River, I cupped her ass, giving it a firm squeeze. "What do you want for dinner?" I asked as I bent to kiss her neck. I knew I was pushing things, but I couldn't help myself.

"I'm good with whatever," she said, leaning into me for all of two seconds before forcing herself to put distance between us.

I muttered a curse, hating that we had to hide our relationship. Plenty of people knew, but not her dad or mine, or any of the older members of the MC. They would kill me if they knew I'd been having sex with River since she was fifteen. It wouldn't matter that I'd only been sixteen when it started.

But the moment she turned eighteen, I was going to beg her father to let me be with her. On my knees if I had to. Not just to let me date her, but to let me marry her. I already had the ring. I made good money, and I had a trust fund my mom had set up for me from the money her dad had left her. I had my own apartment, but I'd been looking at houses for us to buy.

River had her own plans, her own money she could do whatever she wanted with. I didn't care what she did as long as she was happy. She could spend every cent her grandpa Hank left her, because I would always make sure she was taken care of.

"Order us some takeout, baby," I told her, pulling my credit card out of my wallet. "Whatever you want. You know what I like."

"I can pay for dinner," she argued.

I pushed the card into her hand, glaring down at her. "Don't start with me tonight, woman. Order us some food. Ask Dad what he wants too."

"Dad doesn't want anything," he said as he came out of the back, still holding Ian's car seat. Lyric followed them to the front door, waving at River on the way. "I'm going home for dinner later."

River watched them go before looking up at me with a

sultry little look on her beautiful face that made me want to grab her and drag her into the storage room so I could sink balls deep into her. "I want Aggie's for dinner."

"See if Kingston will drop it off, then," I told her just as the front door opened and my next client walked in. I gave the guy a chin lift. "Come on back, man. I've got everything ready to go."

River stopped me when I would have turned away. "Kingston is on a run with Uncle Raider and my dad."

"Then Jack. Have him drop it off."

"Why can't I go pick it up myself?" she muttered with a pout.

"Because I want you here with me." I stroked a finger down her bare arm. "Have someone drop off the food or order delivery from somewhere else. Please?"

"Fine," she said with a roll of her eyes. "But only because I have too much homework to get done to go myself."

"Sure, baby." While the client went on back, I cupped River's ass again and lowered my head, touching my lips to the shell of her ear. "Be good, and we can have dessert before you go home tonight."

"I'm not in the mood for dessert," she sassed, putting distance between us after checking the front door.

"Yeah?"

She nodded, a sly look in her pretty eyes, and I licked my lips in anticipation.

"But I'm starving for it, sweetheart. I can't wait to taste that decadent honey that's just for me."

"Mav," she moaned.

"Later," I promised.

W HILE I WAITED FOR THE FOOD TO ARRIVE, I TEXTED Mila and asked her if we could reschedule meeting the real estate agent. She assured me it wasn't an issue, but of course, she then asked why I couldn't make it.

Instead of answering, I turned off my ringer and finished up my homework.

Uncle Spider's client had already been and gone, and he'd left soon after. He didn't tell me what he was doing that had required me to reschedule, and I knew better than to ask. Most likely, it was something club-related, and he wouldn't have even told Aunt Willa about it, let alone me.

Maverick's third appointment was already in the back with him when a motorcycle pulled up right in front of the shop. I grinned as Elias walked in the door with a bag of food from Aggie's in each hand while giving me a mock glare.

"You're lucky you're a pretty little thing, or I'd charge you for my services," he said as he swaggered toward me. Like his brother Reid, and my cousin Max, Elias looked just like the older Reid generation. Dark black hair, electric-blue eyes, and shoulders as wide as the door. Elias wasn't quite as tall as Max or Reid, but since he worked at Barker & Reid Construction, which his parents owned, he was just as broad as the other two.

"Aw, aren't you sweet?" I said with a roll of my eyes. Elias was nothing but a flirt, but he was one of the few people in my close-net family who wasn't related to me by blood.

I grabbed the first bag he set on the counter and pulled out the top to-go box from Aggie's, not even caring what was inside. Grabbing a fry, I stuffed it into my mouth, feeling like I hadn't eaten in forever. I'd skipped breakfast that morning since I'd been running late, and lunch had been a few carrot sticks because school food was disgusting.

"Thanks for bringing this over," I said, chewing my food. "I couldn't reach Jack or Max, and your brother was still at work."

"Anytime," he assured me, leaning down and putting his elbows on the counter. "I was meaning to stop by here anyway."

I lifted a brow, continuing to stuff fries into my mouth.

"Mom wanted me to ask you what you want for your birthday," he said with a shrug. "She still hasn't gotten you a present, and the party is only a few days away."

Pulling a napkin from the bag, I wiped my fingers before poking him in the chest. "Liar. What you mean is, *you* haven't gotten me a present yet."

"I hate that you can so easily see through my bullshit," he grumbled, then grinned. "Okay, okay. So, I haven't gotten you a present yet. Come one, Riv. Give me a hint, a teeny-tiny clue. I'm shit at buying presents, and you know it."

I rolled my eyes at him. "I don't even care if you give me a present or not. Just come to my party."

"My mom will beat my ass if I show up to the party without a present," he whined. "Please, please, please just tell me so I can get it and be done."

"Fine." I started unbagging the rest of the food, knowing Maverick would be hungry once he was done with his client. "What I really want is an IOU."

"What?" he demanded with a confused frown.

"You heard me. I want an IOU. Basically, if I ever need something, you show up and help me out, no questions asked. And you keep your mouth shut."

He shook his dark head. "And how the fuck do I wrap up something like that to give to you at the party?"

Turning, I picked up a sheet of blank printer paper and a pen. Placing it on the counter, I instructed him what to write and then folded it up and handed it to him. "Now, you put that in a tiny gift box and bring it to the party. I don't have to open it, and Aunt Jos won't murder you for showing up empty-handed."

He put the folded paper in his jeans pocket. "And by anything, you mean..." His brows bobbed up and down suggestively, and I snorted out a laugh.

"Shut up, Elias. If Mav hears you, you know you'll be sucking your meals through a straw for the next six months." Leaning forward, I lowered my voice. "I mean, if I call you and say I need you to move a dead body, your ass shows up and you don't complain. And you sure as fuck don't tell anyone."

"Who are you planning on killing?" There was no concern, just pure curiosity in his eyes.

"You, if you don't shut up," I hissed. "That was just a hypothetical, dummy. I'm not saying I need you to bury a body. But one day, you might get a call that requires you to show up and keep your mouth shut. Understand?"

"Yeah, yeah, sure." He pushed back from the counter. "I have to get home. Call me if you need anything. If not, I guess I'll see you at your party."

"Thanks for bringing my dinner," I called after him with a wave.

While I was alone in the front of the shop, I texted my mom.

Me: *Any news?*

Mom: *Raven and I went to some of the surrounding cities around Oakland today. One woman thought she saw D at a soup kitchen—three fucking weeks ago.*

My heart clenched at the thought of my cousin having to go to a soup kitchen for food. Mom had been searching for Delaney ever since she found out about her niece, but Delaney had run away from her aunt and uncle's house down in Oakland as soon as she'd turned eighteen.

Poor Delaney was out there somewhere, completely alone. Was she cold? Hungry? Scared?

Blinking back the sting of tears, I encouraged Mom to keep looking and not to give up. When I got a heart emoji in reply, I slid my phone into my back jeans pocket and stuffed another fry into my mouth. The rest of the evening flew by, but as I was locking up, Mom showed up at the shop looking exhausted.

"Drive me home," she urged quietly, glancing over my shoulder to make sure Maverick was still in the back. "Raven dropped me off since your dad is home, and I don't want him asking questions about where I was all day. If he thinks I was here with you all evening, he won't question me."

I pushed down my disappointment that I wouldn't get to stay and give Maverick his anticipated dessert. But if I expected my mother to cooperate with me when I needed her to, I had to help her out a little, too. "Okay, but tomorrow, I have somewhere to be. Cover for me with—" I nodded toward the back "—and Dad."

Her eyes narrowed on me. "Where do you have to be, little girl?"

Jaw clenched, I remained mute, just looking at her and daring her to question me further. If she wasn't going to confide in Dad about what was going on with her and finding Delaney, I didn't have to tell her what was going on with me just yet.

"Fine," she muttered, blowing out a frustrated sigh. "I get it. And yes, I'll cover for you."

"Thank you," I whispered. "Give me two minutes, and I'll be ready to go."

"Hurry."

I walked into the back to grab my backpack and purse from Maverick's room. He was cleaning the space, getting everything ready for his first appointment the next afternoon. When he saw me pick up my things, he grabbed my hips. "Where do you think you're going?" he growled, lowering his head to kiss my neck.

I leaned into him, savoring his lips on me. "I have to go." I stroked my hand over the scruff on his jaw, wishing I could stay and just let him hold me. "Mom is out front waiting on me. Something came up, and I need to take her home."

Disappointment filled his gray eyes, but he nodded in understanding. "Okay, baby. Just be careful." He brushed his lips over mine. "Love you, River."

"Love you, Mav," I whispered before forcing myself to step back.

He followed me to the front, stopping to hug my mom before we walked out the door and he locked up behind us. I tossed my things into the back seat while Mom got into the passenger seat. By the time I got behind the wheel, only a few seconds had passed, but she already had her head leaned against the window and was drifting off to sleep.

Sighing, I leaned over and fastened her seat belt before driving us home.

Dad didn't even question her when we walked into the house fifteen minutes later. Sometimes, if Mom didn't help out at the bar, she would come and keep me company at the shop, so it wasn't unusual for us to come home together.

Leaving my parents in the kitchen, I went upstairs to get ready for bed. After showering, I texted Maverick good night and that I loved him, something I did every night, no matter what. Just as I started to drift off to sleep, my phone pinged with his message.

Maverick: *Sweet dreams, baby. Love you.*

My eyes filled with tears, and I cried myself to sleep.

THE DRIVE back to Creswell Springs felt like it took forever the next evening. I was exhausted from traveling to a city I didn't know on top of everything else.

That morning, I'd called Aunt Willa to let her know I wasn't feeling well so I wouldn't be able to work that evening. She'd told me she would handle the shop for me and hoped I felt better. I hadn't gone to school that morning, but Mom knew I wasn't going and had agreed to cover for me with everyone. If Maverick came looking for me, she'd promised she would tell him I was in bed sleeping.

Once I was home again, I went straight up to my room and showered the day off me. My heart felt so heavy, and I could barely keep my eyes open as the water rained down on me, mixing with my tears.

I'd thought I could be brave and do what had to be done on my own, but the truth was, I was a scared little girl. I'd chickened out at the last minute and run.

I loved Maverick more than life. All I wanted to do was protect him, but I couldn't do what I knew I needed to do to ensure nothing happened to him. Not this time...

Now I had to face the consequences and pray everything would be okay.

As I washed my body, I saw the small bruise and tiny pinprick mark on the inside of my arm where the IV had been. The nurse had been seconds away from giving me the medication that would sedate me when I'd freaked out and jerked the needle out of my arm. I'd grabbed my clothes and gotten the hell out of there.

Holding back a sob, I touched a trembling hand to my flat belly. "I'm sorry," I whispered. "I'm so sorry. I love you. I do. But I love your daddy too. I thought if I... That..." I clenched my eyes closed and sucked in a deep breath. "I just didn't want them to kill him. But in the end, I couldn't. I haven't even met you yet, and I love you more than I've ever loved anyone. Maybe even more than Maverick."

I'd never thought that was possible. That I could love anyone as much as I loved him. But this was a different kind of love. This was a feeling that came straight from the marrow of my bones. There was life growing inside me that I'd created with my soul mate. Part of Maverick was sleeping right under my heart.

I'd been minutes away from ending my pregnancy,

because I knew that was the only way to truly protect Mav from my father.

But I couldn't.

I couldn't choose between the man I loved and the baby that already owned my heart.

FOUR
MAVERICK

My alarm woke me at noon, telling me it was time to get my ass up and start the day. Groaning, I turned it off and just lay there for the longest time.

There was a pressure in my chest that was alien to me. A heaviness that kind of hurt—only it wasn't an actual physical ache. It felt deeper, and I didn't understand it.

Rubbing my hand over the spot that seemed to ache the most, I reached for my phone to text River. This time of day, she was in class, but she typically kept her ringer off, so I knew texting her wouldn't get her into trouble.

Me: *I think I need a hug.*

Rolling my eyes at what a pussy that made me seem like, I got out of bed and walked into my kitchen to start a pot of coffee. I'd moved out of my parents' house right after my sisters got married. My apartment was a small one-bedroom, but I didn't need much space.

That would change when River moved in. though, and I knew I needed to find us somewhere bigger to show her dad that I could take care of his baby girl the way she deserved. Scrubbing a hand over the scruff on my face, I pulled up the local real estate sites to see if something bigger was available for rent.

When I didn't see anything I knew my girl would like, I groaned and texted River again.

Me: *Maybe we should just buy a small house for now. Like a starter house or something. Check out the site and let me know if you see anything you like, baby.*

I included the real estate site I'd been looking at, but when the message went unread, I figured she was just busy with class.

While I got ready for work, that heavy feeling in the middle of my chest only intensified, making me feel sick to my stomach. The fact that my texts to River were still unread was only making the sensation worse. When I got to work and saw that her car wasn't where it should be, I nearly puked in the parking lot.

Something was wrong. My girl wouldn't torture me by not answering my messages and then being late for work without a reason. In my gut, I knew something was wrong.

Fuck, I'd known something was off with her for a few weeks, but every time I'd asked her what was going on, she would just say she was worried about what was going to happen on her birthday. No matter how hard I tried to reassure her I would handle the dads, I hadn't been able to alleviate her fears.

Seeing my mom's SUV in the parking lot, I walked into the shop to see if she knew what was wrong with River.

Mom didn't handle the shop often. Like River, she got jealous as fuck when Dad had to ink some chick, and it was just better for everyone if she wasn't around. That was why I was all for River opening a store with my sister.

"Hey, honey," she greeted from behind the counter where she sat, looking bored to tears.

"Hey," I muttered, bending to kiss her cheek. "River meeting Mila and the real estate agent?"

"No, she called me this morning and said she was sick..." I was already on my way back out of the door. "Mav, you have an appointment in two hours," she called after me. "If you aren't here for it, your dad is going to wonder where you are."

"I have to make sure she's okay," I told her from the door.

Her eyes softened. "Just be back before your appointment, or James is going to ask questions. He's not stupid, Maverick. With River out sick and you not here, he will put two and two together."

"I'll try to be back in time, but I can't make any promises. If she's not feeling well, I'm not leaving her alone."

"The girl needs rest," she tried to argue.

"My girl needs *me*," I growled before jogging to my motorcycle.

It was a fifteen-minute drive to River's house. On the way, I passed her dad's bar and saw his bike in the parking lot. Glad I wouldn't have to deal with him, I sped to her place.

Kelli was home, however, but when I knocked on the door, she was all too ready to let me in. Her face was tight as she stepped back, her gaze going to the stairs. "She's not feeling too great right now, Maverick. I'm not sure what she's got, but I've heard her crying for the past hour or so. When I went in to check on her, she wouldn't tell me what's wrong."

The pressure in my chest only increased, and I practically ran up the stairs to River's room. I didn't bother knocking, just pushed her door open. When I heard her sniffling under her covers, I closed the door quietly and then kicked off my boots before climbing into bed behind her.

As soon as my arms were around her, she turned over and burrowed herself against me. Her pitiful little sniffles turned into body-quaking sobs as her fingers dug into me.

"Baby, what's wrong?" I asked, my voice choked with emotion because I'd never been able to take River's tears. When she hurt, I hurt.

"Please...just...hold...me," she sobbed, clinging to me tighter.

Cupping the back of her head in one hand, I rubbed her back with the other while her tears soaked my shirt. I just lay there, holding her and letting her cry it out. I didn't know what was wrong, but I vowed to make it better, no matter what it took.

When her sobs turned into heart-wrenching little hiccups, I lifted her head so I could see her face. Even with her eyes red and swollen, her face drowning in tears, and snot running out of her nose, she was still the most beautiful girl I'd ever seen. Using my thumb, I wiped some of her tears away. "You ready to tell me what's wrong, baby?"

Her lashes lowered, causing a few more tears to squeeze out of her troubled eyes. "Do... Do you promise not to hate me if I tell you?"

"There is nothing you could do that would ever make me hate you," I told her truthfully.

"Today..." She broke off and pressed her face into my chest again. "Today, I drove up to Oregon. To... To... But I couldn't do it, Mav. I couldn't."

I tensed. "Couldn't do what?"

"Oh God," she moaned, but her voice was muffled as

she pressed against me. "Please know I love you. You are my everything. I would give up everything for you. But I couldn't put you first this time."

Heart pounding, I rolled her onto her back. Cupping her face, I held her in place and lowered my head until we were only inches apart. "What couldn't you do, River?" I demanded.

Her body began to tremble, and she took my hand from her face. After kissing my palm, she lowered it until we were both cupping her lower abdomen. "I-I'm pregnant," she whispered.

My heart did a funny little flutter in my chest, and my eyes stung with tears. "You are?" I choked out, in awe of what she was saying.

I knew it was a given that we would eventually have kids, but they hadn't been on my mind. With her telling me it was happening sooner rather than later, however, emotions I couldn't describe filled me.

Her tears began to flow once again. "Y-yes."

"Baby, that's... Fuck." I kissed her, hard, my entire body vibrating with love for her and the life that was growing in her belly.

But she pressed against my chest, breaking the kiss. "It's not a good thing, Maverick!" she cried. "This is going to get you killed."

"You're overreacting," I tried to assure her, but deep in my gut, I knew she had reason to be concerned. Still, I didn't want her to worry.

"Listen to me!" she commanded, sitting up and leaning back against the headboard. Pressing her hands to her face, she gave a muffled scream before scrubbing away her tears. "I went up to Oregon to have an abortion."

"Shut up," I barked, refusing to believe she could ever

do that. "You didn't get rid of our baby."

"No," she whispered, her hands going to her stomach protectively. "I didn't. But I was going to. All I could think was that I had to get rid of... I was so scared—am so scared— that my dad will kill you once he knows. So, I made the appointment, and I went. I-I got as far as the IV when I realized I couldn't. I love our baby so much, Maverick. I-I couldn't..."

"Why didn't you tell me?" I demanded, pissed at her— and a little at myself for not paying more attention. For not making her tell me what was wrong when I knew fucking good and well there was something up with her.

"Because I didn't want you to feel guilty." She shifted her gaze to the window. "Fuck, Mav. I have enough guilt for the both of us. And I didn't want you to worry. I thought...if I just got rid of it, we would be okay. You would be safe."

I grabbed her around the neck, not hard enough to hurt her, but with just a little pressure to make her look at me. She didn't even flinch, my touch grounding her. "This shit ends here, River. You don't ever keep anything from me again. No matter what it is, we face everything together." She opened her mouth to argue, but I tightened my hold. "Am I clear?"

After a small hesitation, she gave a nod. "I'm sorry."

I pulled her onto my lap. "If you're saying sorry because you kept this from me, I forgive you. If you're sorry for anything else, you don't need to be." Stroking her hair back from her damp face, I tilted her face up and kissed her lips. "I don't want you worrying about anything. I'll take care of it."

"H-how?"

"I don't know yet," I told her honestly. "But I promise you, baby, we'll figure it out."

"Are you eighteen or eight?" Nova muttered beside me as we stood in the middle of Hannigans', watching all the dads put up frilly pink decorations.

Dad and Uncle Jet were standing on ladders, hanging a banner that read "Happy Birthday, Princess" in glittery pink and purple lettering.

"Huh, I did have one just like that at my eighth birthday party." Shaking my head, I glanced down at my baby cousin. With her blond hair and eyes the same shade of green as my own, she could have passed for my sister. Only where my features came from my mom, Nova's were all our aunt Raven. "Dad always goes a little overboard on my birthday. I blame it on him having only one kid."

"Please. It's a Hannigan thing," she grumbled. "Did you see my dad at my last birthday party back in November? They got a bouncy castle. I turned thirteen, not six."

"Hey, I had a blast bouncing around in that huge thing," I told her with a grin.

"Because you were the only one in there jumping. None of the kids from school who came would even go near the thing." She pressed her lips into a tight line. "All the girls were too busy drooling over Ryan."

I draped an arm over her shoulders. "Like he would ever give any of them two seconds of his precious time." Which was the truth. Ryan Vitucci hadn't even seen all those girls practically begging for his attention as they stood around him like he was a celebrity. His entire focus had been on Nova and making sure she was happy.

Ryan and Nova's relationship was...weird to me. From the time she was three and he was eight, they had been best friends. There was a connection there that not even the distance from Creswell Springs to New York City could interfere with. But I always figured that once Ryan started getting older, things would change.

Oddly, they hadn't.

When he got to the age when it was normal for a boy to start noticing girls, he'd seemed immune. Everyone began to wonder if maybe Ryan was gay, but he didn't seem to be into guys either. No, it was more like that part of himself was being suppressed.

As if he was waiting...

For Nova to grow up.

Which was adorable, but Nova was only thirteen to his nearly nineteen. He was going to be waiting for a long, long time if that was the case. But I figured that if anyone could do it, it was Ryan. I'd never met anyone as stubborn or as determined as he was, which was saying a hell of a lot considering who my family was.

"River, Nova," Aunt Raven called from behind the bar. "Girls, can you finish getting the food out of the back of my SUV, please?"

"No problem, Aunt Raven," Nova assured her as we headed for the door.

Outside, there were only a few other cars and a couple motorcycles. Raven's black SUV was parked right beside the entrance with the trunk open. There were enough boxes of food platters to feed an entire army, but probably would barely put a dent in the appetites of everyone coming to my birthday party.

I reached the trunk first and picked up the first box, but as I lifted it and turned, a wave of dizziness hit me so hard, I dropped the box.

"Whoa!" Nova caught me around the waist when I began to sway. She was a tiny little thing, but oddly strong as she half picked me up and leaned me against our aunt's vehicle.

Sweat began to bead on my forehead and upper lip. The world was still dim around the edges, and my heart was pounding hard against my ribs.

"Are you okay?" she demanded, touching her hand to my forehead. "You're ice-cold, River, but sweat is pouring off you."

I shook my head, trying to clear it, but that only made my dizziness worse. "Fuck," I whispered, frantically glancing around, but thankfully no one was outside but the two of us.

"Why do you look so freaked out?" my cousin demanded.

"Because..." My eyes went to the front entrance of the bar and stayed there, praying my dad stayed inside until the world stopped spinning. Only one other person knew about my condition and that was Maverick, but I knew Nova would keep my secret. "I'm pregnant."

"Oh," she muttered. "Okay, yeah, I can see why that would be reason enough to be worried. But you're obviously sick right now. You need to go sit down."

"No. Just give me a second. I'll be okay." Bending, I put my hands on my knees and lowered my head, breathing through the nausea that was making the dizziness even worse.

"You stand here. I'll take this inside so Aunt Raven doesn't come looking for us." Nova stepped away, and it was only then that I realized she'd still been holding on to me and supporting a good portion of my weight. At the loss of her stability, I felt like I was going to fall again. Reaching behind me, I braced myself against the SUV a little better so I didn't face-plant into the ground.

Nova picked up the box I'd dropped and hurried inside, appearing again only a moment later. "Still okay?" she asked softly as she grabbed another box.

All I could do was nod because if I spoke, I knew I was going to vomit. The look the younger girl gave me was skeptical, but she carried the next box inside.

I stood there for a couple minutes while she took a few more loads. Just as Nova entered the bar for the fourth time, the sound of a vehicle pulling into the parking lot caught my attention, and I slowly turned my head to see who it was.

Monroe's husband parked their gigantic SUV, and Maverick's youngest sister got out with a beaming smile on her face. Her hair was pulled up into a simple ponytail that hung past her shoulders, and she was wearing a pretty floral dress that clung to the curves she'd kept after having her beautiful baby girls. "Hey, River!" she called as she opened the back door to grab one of the car seats her twin daughters were strapped into.

"H-hey," I called back.

Gian walked around to take the car seat from her. "I told you I would get them, precious," he gently scolded her before dropping a kiss on her lips. "Go speak to the birthday girl. I've got our angels."

Without arguing with him, she practically floated over to me. But when she got close enough, her eyes widened in concern. I tried to give her a small smile, but it felt wobbly, and it only made her that much more worried for me. "Are you sick?"

I lifted a finger to my lips when her voice rose, and she clamped her mouth shut in understanding.

"Where is Mav?" she whispered.

"He had to go on a run to Reno Friday night with Jack and Kingston." I wiped my upper lip with the back of my hand. "He should have gotten back last night, but something came up. He promised he would be back today, though."

I was kind of hoping he wouldn't get back in time for the party, however. I knew it was only putting off the inevitable, but one more day of peace wouldn't have been a bad thing. I wouldn't have to worry about blood being shed at my birthday party—or Maverick being beaten into a coma.

Just thinking of what could happen to the man I loved when he showed up at the party only made my stomach cramp painfully. Whimpering at the sudden agony, I bent in half once again and lost the fight to hold back the vomit.

"Crap," I heard Nova mutter as she ran up to join Monroe. "I knew you wouldn't last long."

I could barely hear her as I retched over and over again, all while trying to stay upright. Eventually, my stomach calmed down enough for me to catch my breath, and with Monroe and Nova on either side of me, I was able to stand upright.

"It sucks that you're sick on your birthday," Monroe soothed. "I heard there was a stomach bug going around."

"Yeah," Nova agreed, her face completely serious, without showing so much as a flicker that she knew my secret. "I think half my first period class had it on Friday."

"Girls, what's taking so long...?" Aunt Raven's voice trailed off when she saw the puddle of puke at my feet while Nova and Monroe held on to me. "Damn. That bug hit you hard." She came over to take Monroe's place and pulled my arm over her shoulder. "Let's get you cleaned up."

"I-I'm okay now," I tried to assure her as she took most of my weight, instructing Nova to finish carrying everything inside so Aunt Flick could put everything out on the bar top.

"I bet you are," she murmured quietly as she helped me to the bathroom.

I glanced around, but it seemed that Dad was either in the office or had gone out the back door to get more decorations. In the bathroom, Aunt Raven locked the main door and then helped me over to the sink. Turning on the faucet, she grabbed a few paper towels and dampened them before wiping my face.

"It shouldn't be called morning sickness if you're ill all day."

My entire body turned to ice, and I knew I had a deer-caught-in-the-headlights look on my face as I lifted my gaze to hers. "I don't—"

"Don't lie to me," she warned, crossing her arms over her chest. "I know a pregnant woman when I see one."

Tears instantly started spilling from my eyes. "Please don't tell Dad," I begged.

Her face softened. "Of course I won't, River. I know this might be hard to believe, but I've been in your shoes."

"I doubt it," I mumbled to myself as I cupped my hand under the faucet and washed my mouth out.

Her laugh echoed off the bathroom walls. "It's the truth. Bash and I snuck around for months without telling any of my brothers we were together." Her face darkened, and she shivered at the memories. "Then they all found out, and Jet beat him so badly..."

"Oh God," I whimpered, my knees going weak. "Maverick is going to die, isn't he?"

"No!" she told me, steel in her voice. Grasping my arms in a firm hold, she gave me a gentle shake until I lifted my head. "I won't let that happen, River. But you have to trust me. I only want to protect you and Maverick, so you have to have a little faith in me. In all of us. Your mom, Willa, and I, we won't let anything happen to either of you. I swear it."

What little color there might have been in my face drained. "Mom and Aunt Willa know that I'm pregnant?"

"Not as far as I'm aware," she assured me. "But we suspected Maverick would probably tell Colt today. We've been preparing for this day. As for your pregnancy... Maybe you should hold off a little while before you make any announcements regarding that joyful news."

I knew if anyone could make this situation less volatile, it was Aunt Raven. Her husband might have been the Angel's Halo MC president, but she was the queen of our family. She ruled us all, and we put our love and faith in her. If she said she would take care of something, I believed her.

But not everything was in her control.

SIX

RIVER

AFTER CLEANING UP IN THE BATHROOM, I FELT somewhat better. By the time Aunt Raven and I walked out, Nova had helped her mom set up all the food, and more people had arrived at the party.

"Drink some lemon-lime soda," my aunt encouraged quietly beside me so only I could hear her. "And then eat a few crackers. Nothing too heavy. It should help with the nausea. Take it easy. Your blood pressure seems to be giving you some issues." She paused at the bar and frowned down at me. "Have you been to a doctor yet?"

I shook my head. The only doctor I'd seen so far was the one at the abortion clinic, but I wasn't about to admit to that. I still felt guilty over even walking through the doors of that place.

"Don't worry. We'll get you in to see one soon," she said with a grim smile, pushing a few strands of my hair out of my face. "Now, go sit. I'll have someone bring you a drink and the crackers."

I walked over to one of the round tables and sat down. No sooner had my ass hit the chair than I was surrounded by a group of guests. I put on a bright smile and greeted them all, thanking them for coming. Fortunately, none of them lingered or sat with me. I was already tired of pretending to be okay.

Nova brought over a cup of soda along with a plate of crackers and a few grapes. "How are you feeling?" she asked as she took the seat beside me. Her eyes scanned my face before relaxing. "You have more color in your cheeks."

"I'm okay now." Picking up the cup, I sipped at the fizzy lemon-lime drink.

"Happy birthday!"

I lifted my head as Mila practically skipped toward me, her long black hair bouncing around her shoulders. Bending, she wrapped an arm around my neck and kissed my cheek. "Happy birthday!" she repeated happily. "Guess what?"

Her excitement had me smiling. "What, Mil?"

"We got the store!" she squealed. "And we can start working on it tomorrow."

"Really?" Laughing, she nodded, and I jumped to my feet, throwing my arms around her. "This is great."

"I knew it would make you happy."

I was glad my arms were still around her, because the world went dark around the edges again, and I went limp against my best friend. She stumbled back, her arms tightening around my waist as she took my weight. "Shit," she hissed. "Are you okay?"

I shook my head. "Give me a second," I whispered. "Please don't drop me."

"Oh my God." She pulled her head back to look at me, her gray eyes wide and full of sudden fear. "Are you pregnant?" she mouthed the words, and all I could do was nod. "Shit, shit, shit."

A few moments went by before my vision completely returned and I was able to step back. But Mila grabbed my hands. "Are you okay?"

I shrugged, unable to answer that particular question. I didn't know if I was okay or not. Nor did I know if I ever would be again, because this was uncharted territory for me. There were too many factors, too many unknowns, and too many dangers for me to have faith there would be a good outcome from this pregnancy.

Lyric walked over to us, a car seat in each hand and a huge diaper bag tossed over one of his shoulders. "Happy birthday, River," he said, kissing the top of my head.

I put a smile on my face. "Thank you." Bending, I stroked a finger down Isaac's and Ian's soft cheeks. "How are my two favorite demon spawn?"

"Ian is grumpy today," Mila informed me. "I think he might have a tooth coming in or something going on with his ears."

"That doesn't sound like fun," I murmured, stroking my thumb over his cheek again. He grunted at me and grabbed my thumb, pulling it into his mouth and biting down.

"No offense, River," Monroe said as she joined us. "But if you have a stomach bug, you shouldn't be letting Ian munch on your fingers."

I quickly pulled my hand away from the baby, only to have him yell up at me in disapproval. I stood slowly, and Mila hugged an arm around my waist, steadying me in case I got dizzy again.

Mila grabbed her twin and pulled her in closer. "She doesn't have a bug," she told Monroe.

"But she was just—"

Mila pinched her side. "Shut up and think about it for a second, Mon."

Monroe pinched her back. "Don't pinch me, Mila. We're not little girls anymore..." Her voice faded as realization hit her, and she turned wide eyes on me. "You're...?"

I turned away from her and picked up my cup of soda from the table where Nova was still patiently sitting. I hadn't planned on telling anyone about my condition that day, but I'd already spilled the secret to four different people now. If I wasn't careful, the entire bar was going to know before the party actually started.

Behind me, I heard Mila and Monroe whispering to each other, but I couldn't make out what they were saying, although I knew it was about me. Lyric used his foot to pull out two chairs from the table and set the car seats in them, pretending like he hadn't heard what his wife and sister-in-law were discussing. Ian was getting fussy, so Lyric unfastened him and lifted his son into his arms.

Seeing the huge man with the baby in his arms had every woman in the room swooning except for Nova and me. A group came over, cooing and baby-talking to Ian while flirting with Lyric. Which had Mila breaking away from her sister and pushing in between the other women and her husband to get to her son.

Bending, she lifted Isaac into her arms. "Anyone want diaper duty?" she snipped at the group.

They quickly scattered, causing Nova to giggle.

"That's what I thought," Mila muttered with a glare around the room.

For the next hour, the bar filled up with more and more guests, but I stayed close to my table. I was thankful everyone wanted to celebrate my birthday with me, but I was torn between wanting Maverick there and hoping he got delayed and missed the party completely.

At seven o'clock, my parents brought out the cake, a

multilayered confection with pink frosting with glittery-purple sprinkles on top. "Happy Birthday, Princess" was written across the bottom tier with eighteen candles already glowing brightly.

I walked over to my parents as everyone sang "Happy Birthday." Mom winked when I rolled my eyes at her, making me smile. I knew she hadn't had a single part in picking out the cake. Dad had always forced pink on me, but if he'd taken two seconds to stop and ask me, he would know that my favorite color was blue.

He was a great father...he just didn't seem to know the real me. He'd come to all my school events, celebrated my every victory and accomplishment academically and regarding the few sports I'd played over the years. But he'd never actually sat down and had a heartfelt conversation with me.

And while part of me was kind of glad he was so oblivious, another part of me wished he'd taken a little time to find out what made me tick. Maybe then I wouldn't be so scared of him finding out about my relationship with Maverick. If he'd just taken a moment to find out what made me happy and accepted the little things instead of just assuming, I would have gladly confided everything in him.

Mom took my hand and tugged me between her and Dad. They both put an arm around me as the song came to an end.

"Make a wish, princess," Dad encouraged, a huge grin on his face.

I looked up at him, praying that he wouldn't break my heart, before bending and wishing for the same thing as I blew out the candles.

Around me, everyone cheered and clapped their hands while Mom kissed my cheek and then Dad hugged me. I held on to him a little tighter for a moment before I stepped back, and Mom started cutting everyone a slice of cake.

I was given the first slice and, after picking up a fork, returned to my table where Nova was still sitting. She might have been years younger than me, but her presence had always calmed me for some reason. Nova had always seemed so much wiser than she should have been for someone so young. As if she could see through anyone and easily read if they were good or bad, and it made me trust her judgment on things.

I sat beside her and offered her my fork, my stomach turning as I glanced at the door yet again. When the one person I wanted to see the most didn't magically appear, I slumped down in my chair, only partially relieved that he hadn't arrived.

Nova took a small bite of the cake then licked her lips. "My dad must have helped Uncle Colt pick out the cake. This is my favorite."

I gave her a tiny smile, but before I could respond, she was squealing and jumped to her feet. I barely blinked, and she took off at a full-on run. Just as she jumped, I saw who was waiting there to catch her. Nova wrapped her legs around Ryan's middle, and he spun her around until she giggled and begged him to stop, while Tavia and Theo laughed and walked around them, their baby girl tucked against Theo's chest.

"What are you doing here?" she cried.

"I was invited," he told her with a deep laugh. "Do you not want me here? I can go if—"

She slapped her hand over his mouth. "No, no, no. I want you here."

Watching them together, I felt my heart lift at the pure happiness on both of their faces. Ryan's dark eyes were bright as he listened to whatever his best friend was excitedly saying, his gaze glued to her adoringly. There was no lust in Ryan's eyes. No heat in how he looked down at her. Those feelings weren't part of their relationship—yet, maybe not ever—although I knew Nova was crushing on him pretty hard.

"You know those *Twilight* movies you made Reid and me watch when you were younger?"

I lifted my head to find Max standing over me with a huge slice of cake on his plate. I'd made him, Reid, and even Elias watch a lot of movies with me when I was little. They would always whine and complain about it, but they would watch them with me, regardless. *Twilight* just happened to be one franchise I'd made him watch repeatedly because I'd been Team Jacob. "What about them?" I asked with lifted brows.

"It's just, when I see Nova and Ryan together, it reminds me of that Jacob guy and the little vampire girl with the weird name." He took a bite of his dessert then pointed his fork in the direction of our cousin. "It's like he imprinted—or whatever you call it—on her."

I glanced back at them and laughed when I realized he was right. "That's adorable."

"That's weird as fuck," he argued.

"Shut up, Max." I picked up the fork Nova had been eating with and stabbed him in the stomach with it. But the damn thing was plastic, and his stomach was rock hard, causing the teeth of the fork to break off and fall to the floor.

"Ouch!" he whined. "That hurt, River."

"Sure it did. Pussy."

"I see it's turning into a bloodbath over here," Elias snarked as he joined us. He dropped down into Nova's seat with his own plate of cake. "Hey River, you have a little something…" He touched his finger to the tip of my nose. "Right there."

I swatted his hand away, already smelling the sickly-sweet icing he'd smeared on the tip of my nose. "Asshole." Picking up a napkin, I wiped the hideous pink frosting away while he laughed.

Max took the free seat on the other side of me. "Have you had a good birthday?"

I shrugged. "So far, so good."

"I got you a gift card as a present," he told me with a smirk as he took another gigantic bite of cake. "Act surprised."

Rolling my eyes, I sat back in my chair and people watched for a few minutes, while Max and Elias talked over my head. My mom was still cutting cake for people, while Dad was standing at the bar with Uncle Hawk, Uncle Bash, and Uncle Spider, who was holding a cranky baby Ian. They looked deep in discussion about something serious from the tense looks on their faces, but I figured it was club-related.

Across the room, Monroe was sitting with her mom as they ate cake, while Gian held one of their daughters against his shoulder, gently burping her. Lyric sat a few feet away with Mila on his lap, while Isaac lay on a blanket at their feet with Monroe's other daughter. The two of them were on their stomachs, grunting at each other, making Mila grin down at them.

Lexa was feeding Finn dessert from her own plate while her mom stood beside her. Ben stood behind his wife with Theo, the two of them already chatting, and Tavia spoke animatedly with the two women. As they spoke, Lexa clapped her hands in excitement as Tavia and Raven hugged tightly. Tavia was one of the family, as much a daughter to my aunt as Lexa was. Rai adored just as much as Finn.

The dull roar of voices echoed through the bar, telling me everyone was having a good time.

A tingle at the base of my spine alerted me the moment Maverick walked through the door. My heart began to pound against my ribs before my gaze even landed on him. Swallowing the lump that suddenly filled my throat, I lifted my head, looking right into those gray eyes that I loved so damn much.

The hunger and love that greeted me only had my heart rate increasing, but he wasn't walking in my direction. He was headed straight for my dad and his own. Blindly, I reached out, my hands grabbing hold of Max and Elias, causing the two of them to stop talking and follow my gaze.

"Shit," Max groaned.

Around the room, everyone stopped talking as their attention was pulled to my boyfriend and father, until all I could hear was the sound of Maverick's booted steps and the blood rushing through my ears.

"Hey," Uncle Bash greeted him. "How did everything go?"

"No problems," Maverick assured him before turning his head to look at my dad. "Sir," he began, only for Dad to laugh.

"'Sir'? What the hell is this? Have you ever called anyone sir a day in your life, kid?" He looked at Uncle Spider. "You finally beat some manners into your son, brother?"

Uncle Spider didn't share his amusement. His dark eyes were glued to his son as Maverick stood before them, and it was as if he were seeing him for the first time. I could see the puzzle pieces finally clicking into place, and he slowly turned his head, looking right at me.

"Please," I mouthed and saw him jerk as if I'd electrocuted him.

Maverick cleared his throat. "Sir, I... I don't know how to say this."

Dad's amusement quickly dried up when he saw how much Mav was struggling. "Just say it."

My heart stood still as the man I loved squared his shoulders and met my dad's gaze fearlessly. "I love River. I humbly ask for your blessing to—"

Dad didn't give him time to finish before he was growling, "No."

"Date her."

SEVEN

MAVERICK

Going on runs was something I was used to, but
I'd been pissed when Reid got stuck on a jobsite and
couldn't go with Jack and Kingston to Reno. When things
had been delayed and we'd had to spend extra time on the
road, I'd nearly blown the whole trip.

I shouldn't have even been there to begin with, and then
it seemed like I was going to miss my girl's birthday. When I
started shaking from the intensity of my rage, the guys we'd
been there to meet had gotten nervous and then hurried shit
along.

Worrying over not arriving in time hadn't kept me from
thinking about what would happen once I got in front of
Colt. The night before in our hotel room, I'd practiced what
I would say to the father of the woman I loved, rehearsing
my speech on two of his nephews.

My plan was to ask for his blessing to marry River.
Might as well let the man know just how committed I was
to his daughter. But Jack had recommended working up to
that and just asking to date her for a while. Throwing
marriage out there right out of the gate was more likely to

end with blood being spilled, which I had to admit was smart. So, I'd amended my speech to just dating.

But nothing I'd rehearsed had come out of my mouth as I'd stood before him.

"I love River. I humbly…"

Humbly? I mentally groaned, surprised that every one of my MC brothers didn't burst out laughing at me being humble. But this was about openly making River mine. I could be humble and anything else Colt Hannigan needed me to be if it meant he didn't stand in my way.

While I was silently berating myself, my mouth kept moving. "…ask for your blessing to—"

"No." His vicious growl cut me off before I could finish speaking.

"Date her."

He took a menacing step toward me, but I stood my ground as he got in my face. Colt was a tall man, but I was a good three inches taller, so we weren't eye to eye as he pushed into my personal space. "No," he repeated. "She's too young to date."

"She's eighteen now," I reminded him, trying to hold on to my anger. He was only a few inches from me. I could feel his breath on my face, could see the tiny red vessels in the whites of his eyes as his agitation started turning his face a puce color. If anyone else had gotten in my personal space like that, I would have already laid them on their ass with a punch to the jaw. But this was River's dad. I couldn't hit him. "I love her, and she loves me. We want to be together."

"What part of 'no' don't you understand, boy?" Colt seethed. "I don't want you near my little girl. You're not—"

"What?" my dad snarled behind him. I shifted my gaze to him to see he was holding Ian, but the look on his face was just as intimidating as Colt's. Fuck, I was just surprised he wasn't yelling at me too. He loved River like a daughter. All the women in our family were important to each and every member of the MC, but there was just something about those Hannigan females that got a man's protective instincts engaged on a whole other level. "He's not what, brother?"

Colt's jaw clenched. "Your kid has no business dating mine."

"Why not?" Uncle Bash asked, his brows raised as he looked down at his brother-in-law. My MC prez and godfather defending me made something tighten in my chest. "He's a good kid. Keeps his nose clean and does what he's told when we tell him to do something. The boy has a job and hasn't been in any trouble. From what I've seen, he respects River."

"Doesn't matter. No one is dating my girl. She's too young and—"

"And you're full of shit."

I was getting whiplash from all the new voices entering the conversation. Aunt Kelli squeezed between her husband and me, getting in his face as he'd gotten in mine. Reaching behind her, she pushed at my chest with one hand, silently telling me to back up. "River is eighteen today, you idiot. Eighteen. That makes her an adult. She can do whatever the fuck she wants. If she wants to date Maverick, she can, and there isn't a damn thing you can do about it. The boy had enough respect for you to ask for your blessing, and you turned into a dick."

"She's just a little girl," he argued, his face turning an even darker red, making me wonder how high his blood pressure was at that moment. "River is still in high school."

"She graduates in little more than a month," she yelled at him. "Would you stop for two seconds and just look around you? Our daughter is all grown up, Colt. She's not a baby anymore. This party only proved to me that you haven't faced the reality that she's an adult now." She lifted her hand, waving it at the banner hanging from the ceiling then at what was left of the pink cake. "You told me to let you take care of the party, and look at what you did. This is the same exact setup we had at her eighth birthday. Even that ugly pink cake."

"She loves pink!"

Kelli stopped and inhaled sharply. "Does she?"

"It's her favorite color," he grumbled.

"Dude, it's blue," my dad muttered from behind him.

Some of the reddish-purple color drained from Colt's face, and he turned his head to gape at the enforcer. "No, it's not."

Dad only glared at him. "She's not even my kid, and I know her favorite color is blue. And I know caramel is her least-favorite cake flavor, but you picked that for her birthday cake."

"You spend too much time with her," he snapped. "She can't work at your place anymore."

"Why? Because I know her better than you?" He shifted my nephew in his arms, looking down at the other man with disgust. "She's eighteen. If she wants to keep working for me, she can and will. Just because you don't know shit about your own kid doesn't mean I have to fire her."

I felt River before she even touched me. Her hands trembled as she wrapped her arms around me from behind, her face pressing into the center of my back as she inhaled deeply. I stroked my hands over her bare arms, soothing myself with the feel of her beneath my fingertips. Being away from her the last few days had been agony. I'd been on runs in the past that had taken longer, but she hadn't been pregnant then.

There had been an urgency in me, screaming at me to get back so I could protect my woman and baby.

I ached to pull her around in front of me, kiss the hell out of her, and mark her as mine right there in front of her father. My instinct to protect her, however, had me keeping her behind me.

"You don't know her better than me," Colt raged at my father as he turned fully to face him. From the look on Colt's face, I knew if Dad hadn't been holding Ian, Colt would have probably punched him. "She's my little girl. If I say she can't work for you anymore, then she won't. And she sure as fuck won't be dating your worthless son."

Behind me, I heard River gasp at the same time my mom and both of my sisters started shouting.

"Stop it!" River's cry drowned out whatever they said. She started to pull away, but I tightened my hold on her. Sighing, she kissed my back then tugged herself free before walking around me to face her father. Colt glared at her, but she marched up to him fearlessly. "Maverick is not worthless, and I'm not going to stand around and let you talk about him like that. I love him, Dad. With everything in me, I love him. And I *will* be dating him. You have no say in it. Just like you have no say in where I work. As of today, I'm an adult, and I get to make my own decisions regarding my life."

"Not while you live under my roof!" His voice boomed off the walls, causing Ian to jump and the other babies to start crying.

She tipped her head back, meeting his gaze without flinching. "Then I guess I'm moving out."

"I forbid it."

A humorless laugh left her. "Forbid all you want. That doesn't mean shit to me now." She shook her head at him. "You know, I've always respected you. You've worked so hard and given me so much. Yet right now, I see you have no respect for me in return, Dad."

His jaw clenched shut, and I saw him gritting his teeth. Long moments passed with father and daughter staring each other down, but then River's shoulders slumped and she turned to me with a sad smile. "Let's go," she murmured softly.

I took her hand and tugged her close. She melted against me as her side brushed mine, and we started for the door.

"River, get your ass back here!" Colt roared behind us.

She glared at him over her shoulder. "I'll get my things from the house later."

He took a step forward, but Aunt Kelli got in his way. "Let her go."

"She's not moving out. Where's Ben? Have him arrest Maverick." River stumbled, and she looked up at me with a ghostly white face as fear filled her eyes.

"What for?" Aunt Kelli demanded. "She's eighteen and leaving willingly with him."

My hand tightened around River. Ben probably could arrest me if they knew I'd gotten River pregnant before she turned eighteen. But no one knew she was carrying my baby.

Still, if Colt found out, he would have Ben tossing my ass in jail in a heartbeat.

That wasn't something I was going to worry about at the moment, however. For now, I just wanted to get my girl home.

EIGHT
RIVER

My relief that there hadn't been any bloodshed was so strong that I sagged against Maverick as soon as we were outside.

His arm tightened, and he pulled me closer into him as we walked to his motorcycle. Taking his helmet, he offered it to me and then climbed on. I put it on and got on behind him. As I pressed my front into his back, my arms going around his waist, everything felt right in the world.

That feeling was short-lived as Dad stormed out of the bar with half the party guests right behind him. "Let's go," I told Maverick, and he started his bike.

"River!" Dad bellowed behind me, and I tightened my arms around Mav.

Before Dad could reach us, the growl of the engine vibrated between my thighs and we were moving.

As we rode to Maverick's apartment, I kept replaying everything from the moment he'd walked into the bar. My heart was still pounding from the fear of what could have happened. Uncle Spider's reaction had been so surprising that I wanted to hug him. But while my dad's reaction wasn't exactly as I'd expected since he hadn't started throwing punches, I had no doubt that if Mom hadn't gotten between him and Mav, he would have.

My wish hadn't come true. Dad might not have physically hurt Maverick, but he'd broken my heart, nonetheless. No one would ever be good enough for me in his eyes. Part of me understood that on some level. A father's daughter was the light of his life.

But if I was so special to him, why hadn't he ever taken the time to get to know me?

Maybe I was being overly sensitive from all the pregnancy hormones, but I was beginning to realize there was a difference in his physically being there for all the special events in my life growing up and his being *present*. He might have been there, but it didn't seem like he'd actually learned anything about who I was as a person.

Within ten minutes, we were pulling into the parking lot of Maverick's apartment building. After he turned off the bike, he reached back and helped me off. Slowly, I got to my feet, not wanting to scare him if I moved too quickly and had another dizzy spell. As soon as his legs swung off the powerful motorcycle, he scooped me up into his arms.

"Happy birthday," he murmured, pressing his lips to my temple as he carried me up the steps to the second floor where his apartment was. "Sorry I was late. I'll make it up to you, I promise."

I laid my head on his shoulder. "You're here now, and that's all that matters."

Reaching his door, he shifted me in his arms long enough to hand me his keys. After handing them over to me, he bent his knees so I could unlock the door and then open it for us. Once we were inside, he kicked the door closed and flipped the lock before carrying me through the apartment and straight to his bedroom.

It wasn't the first time I'd been to his place, but my visits had been few and far between because there was rarely time for us to enjoy the comforts of an actual bed. Other than the necessary furniture, the place had always felt empty to me. He'd said it was because it was missing the most important feature—me.

Carefully, as if I were made of delicate glass, he placed me in the center of his bed and then stepped back. Pulling off his cut, he hung it off the closet door before kicking off his boots. While I watched him, enjoying the show of him stripping in front of me, I strained my ears, listening for signs of a motorcycle or anything else that would alert us to my dad having followed us.

Just because we'd made it to Maverick's apartment didn't mean we were in the clear.

When he was down to just his boxers, Mav walked back to the bed. His gray eyes skimmed over me hungrily, making the ache between my thighs intensify. "It's taking everything in me not to devour your right now." He grabbed my ankle and pulled me to the edge of the bed. Dropping to his knees, he started working on getting my jeans off, and I lifted my hips to help him.

The sound of my clothes hitting the floor hadn't even reached me before his mouth was on my pussy. My fingers stabbed through his hair, holding him in place while his tongue spread my lips and then flicked teasingly over my clit. I arched my back off the bed as my body gave in to the pleasure it knew only Maverick could deliver to me.

"So fucking sweet," he growled, making wet, slopping noises against my core. "I've missed this pussy almost as much as I've missed you."

"Maverick, I'm close," I whined. "Please."

"Shh, I got you, baby." Squeezing my ass in his hands, he lifted me closer, but he continued to tease me. With only the very tip of his tongue, he licked from my clit down to my entrance, where he circled and then traveled back to my pulsing clit once more. I felt my arousal dripping down my ass, his torture only turning me on more.

He licked and sucked and teased me until I was begging him to finish me off. Maverick knew all my triggers, and when his thumb circled my rear entrance just as his tongue thrust deep into my center, I screamed his name as my release sent me flying.

I was still struggling to catch my breath when he lifted me to the center of the bed again. Pushing his boxers down, he thrust deep inside my still convulsing pussy.

"Motherfuck," he groaned. "You feel so damn good, baby."

"You...too," I panted, wrapping my legs around his hips. "I missed you so much."

"Ah, babe. I missed you more. Hate being so far away from you, River. Can't breathe when you're not close." He licked up my neck, the edge of his teeth grazing my skin and making my inner walls clench around his thick shaft. "You keep that up, and I'm going to blow before either of us is ready."

"Who said I'm not ready?" I turned my head and caught his mouth. I thrust my tongue into his mouth hard, urging him to pump his hips into me with the same intensity. I was already close again.

And like Mav knew all of my triggers, I knew all of his. We were each other's firsts, and we knew each other's bodies as well—if not better—than we knew our own. While I sucked on his tongue, my nails sliced down his back, giving him that little taste of pain I knew always sent him over the edge.

His cock stretched me even farther as the first shot of his come spilled deep inside me. The feel of his hot release triggered my own, making my walls contract around his hard girth as I milked him of every last drop.

Maverick collapsed on top of me, and I savored the feel of his weight pressing me into the bed. But it only lasted a few seconds before he cursed and rolled onto his side. "Sorry, baby. I didn't mean to squish you and our munchkin."

"You didn't," I tried to assure him, but he only wrapped his arm around my waist and pulled me on top of him as he rolled onto his back.

"I'll be more careful."

My eyes were already closing. I'd barely slept the night before, worrying over what might happen at my party. Now that things were mostly okay—and my body was still humming from sex—my lids became too heavy to hold open.

Maverick shifted, then pulled the blankets up over us. Before I fell asleep, I felt him kiss the top of my head. "Love you, babe."

"Love you," I garbled sleepily.

NINE

RIVER

Dawn was just starting to break when I finally found the strength to lift my lashes. My bladder was screaming in agony, and my stomach was grumbling from lack of food. Groaning, I untangled myself from Maverick's hold and stumbled to the bathroom.

There was a towel on the floor when I walked in. Picking it up, I placed it in the hamper before relieving myself. But as I sat on the toilet, an intense cramp like I had when I was on my period hit me so hard that my arms shot out to steady myself even though I was sitting down. My palms hit the walls on either side of me, and I whimpered as the pain lingered.

Inhaling slowly, I tried to breathe through the cramp, and slowly, it began to fade. When it stopped, the relief of no longer being in pain was almost euphoric. Until I wiped and saw the smear of blood on the tissue paper.

My heart stopped as I looked down at the stark red on white. "No," I whispered, my free hand going to my lower abdomen. "No, it's okay. You're okay."

I told myself it was just a little blood, that maybe Mav

was just too rough when we'd had sex. But that cramp had been close to the one I'd experienced the day before when I'd picked up that box from Aunt Raven's trunk.

Sick with worry, I washed my hands and then walked back into the bedroom. I pulled a pair of Maverick's black boxers out of a drawer and stepped into them before finding a T-shirt in his closet to wear. Maverick was still out cold, so I went into the bathroom to make a toilet paper pad before going to the kitchen in search of a bottle of water and my phone.

My stomach was tossing, and I knew I needed to try to eat something since I'd only had a few crackers the day before. I placed a slice of bread in the toaster and then searched Google for what the spotting and cramps could mean.

Monroe had had the same thing happen to her when she was pregnant, but it had been because she was carrying twins and a vessel had ruptured while her uterus was expanding. With Maverick being a triplet, and his sisters identical with twins of their own, it was obvious multiples ran on his side. I hadn't thought that I could be carrying more than one baby, but it was a huge possibility.

"That's what this is," I muttered to myself. "It's like what happened with Mon. The baby...or babies are okay."

After the toast popped up, I walked into the living room to eat it while I flipped through my phone. I had over twenty texts from Dad waiting on me, and that wasn't counting the fifty missed calls from him. Rolling my eyes, I ignored his texts and skimmed over the ones from Monroe, Mila, Nova, Aunt Raven, Aunt Willa, and my mom.

They all asked if I was okay, told me my dad was pissed, but Mom had made him go home. I was thankful she'd had my back through everything. Even when I thought she was cheating on Dad and I'd been angry with her, I never once doubted that she would put me first. She might not be June Cleaver, but she sure as fuck was a great mom, and I loved her.

It was Monday, so I had to go to school. With only a few more weeks left, I couldn't let anything get in my way to keep me from graduating. The thought of putting on the clothes I'd worn the day before made me cringe, but there wasn't anything of mine at the apartment.

I texted Mila, knowing she was up with one or both of the boys by now, and asked if she would mind bringing me a few of her own clothes over until I could get my things from my parents' house.

Mila: *Lyric will drop them off in 15.*

Relieved that I would at least have something clean to wear to school, I walked back to the bathroom and took a quick shower, not bothering to wash my hair. But as I got out, another cramp hit me. "Fuck," I cried, bending in half from the pain.

Wetness gushed out of me, a few drops hitting the white tiles on the floor and smearing across my thighs. I blanched. This was definitely not just a little spotting now.

I told myself not to panic, but that didn't stop it. Scared, I stumbled naked and wet into the bedroom. "Maverick!" I yelled, my voice trembling from fear and anxiety.

He jerked upright in bed, his eyes wide and alert. "Babe?" When he saw me, he jumped to his feet. "River, what's wrong?"

"I-I'm bleeding. And I've been c-cramping," I stuttered, tears blinding me. "I think...I'm losing the baby."

He picked me up and sat me on the end of the bed. "Give me two minutes," he said, kissing my forehead.

I sat there watching him pull on clothes. He came back

to me with one of his T-shirts and some sweat pants. But before he could help me into them, there was a hard knock on the front door.

"That's probably Lyric," I told him. "Mila was sending me over some clothes to wear to school."

He nodded, helping me into his clothes before picking me up again and carrying me through the apartment. Shifting me in his arms, he opened the door just as Lyric lifted his arm to knock again. There was a small gift bag in one hand that must have held the borrowed clothes, but once he saw the tears streaming down my face and how tense Maverick was, the smile on Lyric's handsome face disappeared.

"What's going on?" he demanded.

"You got your SUV?" Mav barked instead of answering.

"Yeah, but—"

"She's bleeding, man. I need to get her to the hospital."

"No!" I cried, shaking my head frantically. "Not the one here."

"River," Maverick gritted out. "You need medical assistance."

"I know," I sobbed. "B-but we can't go to the hospital here. It will get back to my dad and he'll know and then Ben will arrest you and...and...and..." I was starting to gasp as my anxiety made it harder and harder to breathe. A part of my brain was screaming to calm down, this was just a panic attack, but I couldn't.

Lyric lifted his free hand. "It's okay, River. We'll drive a few counties over."

"Fine," Maverick gritted out. "But if you get worse, we're stopping, no matter how close we are. I'll deal with your dad and Ben if it comes to that. But I'm not going to risk something happening to you, baby."

I couldn't get my voice to work, so I only nodded.

While Maverick carried me down to the SUV, Lyric ran inside to grab Mav's phone and keys since he'd forgotten them. It only took a few minutes, and then we were on the road. Lyric called Mila, telling her what was going on, but when she said she was going to follow us, Maverick convinced her to stay home and cover for me with school and my dad.

Not even thirty minutes into the drive, another cramp hit me. It was so painful, it robbed me of oxygen, and I curled into a ball on Maverick's lap in the back seat. It was only the third cramp of the morning, but each one of them had gotten worse and worse. "Drive faster!" he roared, his fingers trembling as he stroked my hair back from my face. "It's okay, baby. You're going to be fine."

"Th-the b-baby," I cried, burying my face in his neck. I knew in my soul that I was losing the baby. The cramp had pushed more blood from me, and I didn't need to look down to see that it had leaked through the sweat pants and onto Maverick's jeans.

"Shh," he soothed in a choked voice. "Don't think about that."

But how could I not?

Just the week before, I'd nearly aborted our baby. And now I was losing him or her. Guilt engulfed me like a physical vise. Was this my punishment for even thinking of getting rid of something so precious?

Pressed up against Maverick, I felt the vibrations as he spoke, but I was crying so hard I couldn't hear anything he or Lyric said. When we started to slow down, I clung to Maverick. "N-no. We aren't far enough away."

"Shut up, River," he growled, kissing the top of my head.

Moments later, Lyric braked hard, and Maverick threw the door open. Holding me against his chest, he ran into the emergency room and yelled for help. As he laid me on a gurney, another cramp hit me, knocking the air from my body, and I curled into the fetal position as the pain became too much to withstand. It was the worst pain of my entire life, so intense that the world began to go dark around the edges.

Vaguely, I heard someone asking questions, but I couldn't answer as I tried to breathe.

"River Masterson," Maverick was saying. "She's my wife. Please…" His voice cracked, making my heart hurt even more than it already was. "Please, just help her."

I felt the gurney moving, and then someone was stabbing a needle into my arm for an IV line. A doctor started examining me, but other than the feel of her ice-cold hands, I didn't understand much of what was going on. This cramp was different from the others. It was lingering, making it hard to even think about anything outside the circle of agonizing pain.

They must have given me something for the pain through the IV, because suddenly, I felt as if I were floating. I blinked up at the ceiling a few times, the fluorescent lights glaring down at me as if judging me. Maverick was holding on to my hand so hard, my fingertips felt numb.

Then the lights went dim, and I felt something warm and gooey being squirted onto my belly.

"There's the heartbeat," someone said, unknowingly stabbing a knife into my heart. "And here…that's the fallopian tube. It's ruptured, by the looks of it. We need to get her into surgery. Now."

"No!" I screamed at the doctor. "You can't. Y-you just said that there was a heartbeat."

She gave me a sympathetic grimace. "I'm sorry. There's nothing we can do. Right now, your life is the one in danger. You're losing too much blood."

"No, no, no," I whispered. "Maverick, tell them. Make them understand I don't want surgery. I-I'll be fine. Our baby still has a heartbeat. That's all that matters. Tell them!"

I felt his free hand stroke down my cheek, but when he spoke, he broke my heart. "Do whatever you have to," he told them. "Anything to protect her."

TEN
MAVERICK

"*No!*"

River's scream as they wheeled her away for surgery echoed in my head. It was full of grief and anger. But if there was a choice between her life and anyone else's— *anyone's*— I would pick hers every fucking time.

When she was gone, another nurse came up to me, telling me I needed to register River. Feeling like I was in a daze, I followed the woman. I gave them all of her information, but when they asked for her date of birth, I lied and told them she was born a year earlier than she actually was. The woman behind the desk asked about insurance, and again, I lied. Instead, I handed her my credit card and told her to charge everything to it.

I had some money saved, and there was plenty of it in my trust fund. I would dip into that if we needed to.

Once I'd signed all the paperwork, the woman gave me an sympathetic smile. "Hope your wife gets well soon."

Nodding in thanks, I took my copies of the papers and then walked back out to the waiting room.

Lyric pushed away from the wall near the entrance as soon as he spotted me. "Well?"

I rubbed my free hand over my face. "The baby was in her fallopian tube. When it grew too big, the tube ruptured. She's in surgery now."

"Fuck, man. I'm so sorry." He squeezed my shoulder. "Do you need anything?"

"All I need is for her to be okay," I muttered.

"Yeah, man. I understand. If it were Mila—" He broke off, but he didn't need to say anything else. I knew. Fuck, I was feeling it.

The nurse who had put the IV in River's arm came over to us. "The doctor asked me to tell you to wait upstairs in the OR waiting room, and she will come speak to you once your wife is out of surgery."

Upstairs, the waiting room was already pretty crowded with family members of patients also having surgery. Most of them had been scheduled, unlike River's, which was an emergency. Lyric and I found two empty seats near a window and sat, neither of us speaking as we waited.

"Dude, you need me to get you a change of clothes?" Lyric asked after a while. "You've got blood…" He waved his hand at my legs.

Glancing down, I realized he was right. River's blood was all over me. A lump filled my throat, and I fought against the sting of tears. "She has to be okay, Lyric," I whispered, unable to get my voice to go any louder. "If I lose her, I'll lose everything that means anything to me."

One of his heavy hands fell on my shoulder, squeezing hard. "I know, brother. It will be okay. Just have faith in the doctors. Your girl is strong."

All I could do was nod, knowing he was right. River was a strong woman; she wouldn't let anything keep us apart.

Not her dad, and sure as hell not this. But that didn't stop me from being scared out of my mind that something might still take her away from me.

It felt like days passed before the same doctor from the emergency room walked into the waiting room. My eyes were glued to the door, so as soon as I saw her, I was on my feet. Spotting me in the still-crowded room, she walked my way. She had on surgical scrubs, whereas in the ER, she'd only had on regular clothes and the typical white jacket. Her scrubs were damp with sweat, as was the surgical cap she pulled off her head when she reached us.

"Everything went as expected," she said without preamble. "We didn't run into any complications. She's in recovery for now, but she will be put on the labor and delivery floor once she starts to wake up. That should be in about an hour or so."

"But she's going to be okay, right?"

She gave me a sad smile. "Physically, she will be back to normal in no time. Given her reaction to having to have this procedure..." She shrugged. "The recovery time for that isn't something I can give you a time frame for, Mr. Masterson. Just be prepared for her to be...fragile."

Fragile? River?

Those two words didn't go together.

The doctor patted me on the arm. "Someone will be in to show you to your wife's room as soon as she's settled." Her gaze went to my jeans. "Maybe you should clean yourself up before then. Her emotions are going to be scattered, and seeing her blood on you might be a bad idea."

"I'm not leaving." I wasn't stepping foot outside the building until River was able to go with me.

"I got you covered, bro," Lyric assured me. "I think we

passed a mall as soon as we got off the interstate. I'll grab you a change of clothes and pick us up some food."

"Yeah, thanks," I muttered, not caring one way or another. I didn't want to upset River if she saw the blood all over me, but all I could think about was just getting to her. Nothing else mattered but seeing with my own eyes that she was okay, that she hadn't been taken from me.

"Do you have any questions for me?" the doctor asked, looking at me as if she expected me to.

"Will she be able to—" I broke off, not even sure I wanted an answer to the question that was lingering in my head now that the woman had told me my girl was going to be all right.

"Have more babies?" I swallowed hard and nodded. "Her chances have been cut in half, but she's young and healthy. There shouldn't be any reason why she couldn't have another baby—when she's ready."

A little of the pressure weighing on my shoulders eased. Thanking the doctor, I shook her hand, and she promised someone would come to get me soon. As she walked away, Lyric said he was going to go get me a change of clothes and followed her out.

Feeling like I was walking through a fog, I returned to my seat by the window and pulled out my phone. I'd had it on silent so it wouldn't annoy me, but I knew Mila would have been texting me as well as Lyric. I'd seen him sending a message every now and then while we waited, but he'd mostly just been there for me. Even if we hadn't spoken much, just having my brother-in-law there had kept me from losing my mind and trashing the entire room, scaring everyone and no doubt getting myself arrested.

Me: *Hey. She's out of surgery. Just waiting*

for someone to come get me once she's in a room.

Mila: *That's a relief. I was so worried. I called the school and pretended to be Aunt Kelli. Told them she was out sick today.*

Me: *Thanks, Mil.*

Mila: *I wish I were there. I'm so sorry. My heart hurts for both of you.*

I didn't know how to respond to that. My heart hurt too. Now that I knew River was going to be all right, the reality of what we'd lost was starting to hit me. When she'd told me she was pregnant, I'd been so damn happy. It was too soon for us to start a family of our own, but that hadn't mattered to me. I loved that little munchkin so much without even having met him or her.

Now I never would.

I scrubbed my hands over my face as exhaustion and a sadness that felt like it went bone-deep seemed to press me into the chair hard. I loved our baby, but not nearly as much as I loved River. Her life had been in danger, and just the thought of losing her had robbed me of any other course of action. There would be more babies, but there was only one River.

Would she hate me now?

Fuck, I hoped not.

When the doctor said River had to have surgery, she'd stressed that even though the baby still had a heartbeat, it wouldn't be viable for long. At the time, I hadn't even cared. All I could think was that River's life was in danger and a decision had to be made right then, right there.

But there wasn't a decision to make.

Nothing came before River.

Ever.

Lyric returned with a bag of clothes for me, as well as for River, along with two large coffees and a sack of fast food. By the time I'd changed and eaten, a nurse came to get me.

River looked so tiny lying in the hospital bed with a blanket tucked up around her chest. Her face was pale, making the dark shadows under her eyes more prominent. There were wires sticking from everywhere, letting the monitor attached to the wall read her oxygen levels, heart rate, and blood pressure. Her IV line was attached to a few different bags that hung from a pole, supplying her with fluids, antibiotics, and blood.

The nurse gave me an update on River's condition and said she would be out of it for a while with the medication they were given her for pain management and the nausea she'd experienced upon waking from the anesthesia. I nodded like I understood everything the woman told me, but honestly, I didn't take much of it in. It was hard to concentrate on words when the girl I loved more than life was lying there so helplessly.

As the door closed behind the nurse, I dropped into the chair beside the bed and picked up River's hand. Her skin felt chilled, and I bent to breathe a little heat onto her fingers. As I did, I rubbed her index finger with my thumb, only then realizing the ring she always wore there was missing.

She'd only been fifteen when I'd put that ring on her hand, but I'd already known I was going to spend the rest of my life with her.

There weren't many places in Creswell Springs for people to get jewelry, so I'd ordered a ring off the internet. The damn thing had been too big to put on her ring finger, but River had still loved it and put it on her index finger instead, promising me she would never take it off.

Swallowing the lump in my throat, I looked around and spotted it in a clear bag on the bedside table. Still holding her hand in one of mine, I reached for the bag with my other and pulled out the ring. Bending again, I kissed her finger as I slid it back into place, skimming my thumb over the simple platinum heart with the teeny little diamond in the center.

I'd used all the money I'd had saved up to buy that ring, which admittedly hadn't been much since I'd only been sixteen at the time. But the way River had reacted to the sight of the ring had been as if I'd given her one of the crown jewels. Her green eyes had lit up, and the smile that spread over her beautiful face had brought a flame alive deep inside me.

We made love for the first time that day and vowed to each other we would always be together and have each other's backs. No matter what.

A soft moan left her, pulling my gaze to her face. Slowly, her lashes lifted, and she blinked a few times before focusing on me. "Mav?" she rasped out.

"Hey, sweetheart," I murmured. "How are you feeling?"

As I spoke, I saw that reality was returning to her, and she was remembering the events of the morning. Tears filled her eyes, and she tried to tug her hand free from mine. "You...you let them..." Her voice broke off on a sob, and she turned her head away from me.

Lead filled my heart. "Baby, the doctor said there was no other choice."

"I heard the heartbeat."

"I know," I whispered, blinking back my own tears. "I heard it too. It was a sweet sound that I'll never forget."

She turned angry eyes on me. "Then how could you let them take it away from us?"

"Because you were going to bleed to death if I didn't!" River flinched at my raised voice. I cleared my throat and tried to rein in my emotions. "The baby was dying, and so were you. There can be other babies, but there's only one you." I cupped the side of her face with my free hand, wiping away one of her tears with the pad of my thumb. "There wasn't a choice to make. You are my everything."

Her choked sobs were slowly killing me, but there was nothing I could say to make any of this better for her. For either of us.

"Th-this is m-my punishment," she said with a whimper, breaking my heart even more.

I frowned down at her in surprise. "For what, baby?"

"F-for almost...almost..."

I inhaled sharply. "No, River. Sweetheart, no. This isn't your punishment. You didn't do anything wrong."

"B-but I almost did," she choked out.

"Almost doesn't count." I moved to sit on the edge of the bed, turning so I could hold her. As she wrapped her arm around me, some of the tension left both of our bodies, and she pillowed her head on my chest. "You're not being punished. I swear."

"Then, why?"

Pushing her hair back from her face, I kissed her forehead. "You didn't do anything wrong. It was just one of those things. Didn't you hear what the doctor said before they took up to surgery?"

She shook her head. "I was kind of out of it. Between the pain and the drugs they gave me, I didn't really understand a lot of what was going on."

"The baby was growing in your left fallopian tube. As it got bigger, the tube burst."

"D-does that mean we can't have more babies?" she cried.

I kissed her again, wanting to take away the pain I was afraid I was about to cause her. "The doctor said it cuts the chances in half."

"O-oh," she whispered, and I felt her shoulders begin to shake as she started to cry again.

"It doesn't matter, though," I murmured, stroking my fingers through her blond hair, aching to take away all her pain—both the physical and the emotional. "If we have another baby, fine. If we don't, then that's fine too. All that matters is that I have you."

ELEVEN
RIVER

I was released from the hospital early the next morning. Surprisingly, I had little pain since the surgery had been done laparoscopically. I had tiny incisions in my belly button and my bikini line, and that was the only proof that only twenty-four hours before I'd been pregnant.

My heart felt heavy as Lyric pulled up outside of Maverick's apartment. Opening his door, Mav got out and then reached back in to assist me. Thankfully, I had fresh clothes Lyric had gotten for me at the mall the day before, and I'd showered earlier, so at least I didn't feel grungy as I slowly walked up the steps to the second floor. '

As I walked, my head was down, my arms wrapped around myself, trying to hold myself together.

"Why the fuck weren't you at school yesterday or today?"

My head snapped up at the sound of my dad's voice. Fuck, I hadn't seen his motorcycle in the parking lot, so I hadn't even considered he would be up there waiting. Instinctively, I took a step back, putting myself between him and Maverick as he and Lyric walked behind me.

"I-I was sick," I told him. "I've had a stomach bug for the last few days. It's been going around school pretty badly."

"Oh," he muttered. "Yeah, Raven and Nova both mentioned you weren't feeling well Sunday." He thrust his hands into the pockets of his jeans as his green eyes skimmed over my face. "You look like you're still sick, River. Did you at least go to the doctor?"

Swallowing the lump of emotion in my throat, I glared at him. "Why are you here, Dad?"

His jaw clenched, and he shot a dark look at the two men behind me before switching his gaze back to me. "You weren't answering your phone."

"It's been off because I didn't feel up to talking to anyone." Not a lie. I hadn't felt like talking to anyone, not even Mila. She'd texted Maverick every hour the day before, but she knew I wasn't up for chatting, so she hadn't called.

"You could have at least texted me that you were alive," he grumbled.

"Well, as you can see, I'm very much alive. You can go now." I took a step back, knowing Maverick was there, and was rewarded with him putting one of his huge hands on my hip. His heat warmed me, something I desperately needed. "I'd like to go lie down."

Blowing out a harsh sigh, Dad stepped aside. "Call me when you feel better. We need to talk, honey."

"If you're going to threaten Maverick and run your mouth, then I'll pass," I gritted out as I continued toward the apartment door.

"As stubborn as your mother," he muttered as we passed each other.

"More like as stubborn as you," I snipped back.

"True," he said with a hint of amusement in his voice. "I'll drop your car off later."

That surprised me. I'd thought because he'd paid for my car, he wouldn't let me have it since I was moving in with Maverick against his wishes.

"But you have to pay the insurance on it now," he countered.

"I pay the insurance on it anyway," I informed him.

He blinked at me in surprise. "You do?"

I rolled my eyes. "Yeah, Dad. I gave Mom the money every month. She said I didn't have to, but I wanted to. Don't worry, though. I'll get my own tomorrow. I'll also get my own phone plan, too."

He scrubbed his hands over his face. "River…"

"Bye, Dad," I told him as I turned my head away. Maverick unlocked the apartment door, and I nearly sagged in relief.

As soon as I was across the threshold, Maverick and Lyric followed me, and I slammed the door shut before flipping the lock.

"I'll add you to my insurance and my phone plan," Maverick informed me as he touched a hand to the small of my back and urged me toward the couch. "I just need to make a few phone calls, and it will be taken care of, baby."

"No, I'll just get my own," I argued as I carefully sat down.

He crouched in front of me. "I know you're not feeling well right now and your head is all over the place. But please don't fight me on this. We don't have to hide that we're together now. That means we share everything. Including bills. Besides, you'll be on everything of mine as soon as we get married anyway."

My heart gave a little leap at the thought of marrying him. Biting the inside of my cheek, I gave a little nod. "Okay, then."

He squeezed my knee before leaning forward to touch his lips to the center of my forehead. "Get comfortable. I'm going to make you something to eat. Then I'll call Mom and tell her neither one of us will be at work later today."

I sat back, pulling my legs up to stretch out on the couch. "D-does she know?"

His hand gently brushed my hair back from my face. "No, baby. You can tell her whenever you're ready."

Blinking back tears, I gave a little nod, and he and Lyric went into the kitchen. Lyric had stayed with us the night before, sleeping in the waiting room in case either of us needed him. I hoped he knew how much I appreciated everything he'd done for us in the past two days, because I didn't know what would have happened if he hadn't been there to help the day before.

No doubt, Maverick would have freaked out and insisted on taking me to the local hospital, and then all hell would have broken loose.

I heard them talking, but I couldn't make out what they were saying. Sighing, I picked up the remote Maverick had given me and channel-surfed while he fixed me something to eat. I'd barely picked at the hospital food I'd been given that morning, but I wasn't hungry. It was hard to think about food when it felt like my heart was no longer part of my body.

Ten minutes passed before Maverick appeared with a tray that held a sandwich and some soup along with a glass of milk.

"I need to get home," Lyric said as he dropped a kiss on top of my head. "But don't hesitate to call me if you guys need anything."

I gave him a tiny smile. "Thanks, Lyric."

"Anything for you, sweetheart." He gave me a wink, nodded to his brother-in-law, and then went out the door.

Mav placed the tray on my lap. "Eat what you can, baby," he urged when he saw the face I made at the sight of the food. "I know you're feeling bad right now, but you have to keep up your strength so you can heal."

Knowing he was right, and not wanting to worry him, I picked up half of the sandwich and took a small bite. It was good, made exactly the way I liked it, but I couldn't get more than a few bites down.

"Try the soup," he told me as he finished off the sandwich for me. "Just a few spoonsful. For me."

Because I knew it would make him stress if I didn't, I picked up the spoon and ate half the bowl of soup then drank a little of the milk. By the time he was satisfied, I was pushing my limits. I wasn't in a lot of pain, but I was feeling uncomfortable, and he encouraged me to take one of the pain pills the doctor had prescribed for me.

Once I'd swallowed it, he picked me up and carried me into the bedroom. After helping me change into one of his T-shirts and a pair of his boxers, he tucked the covers up around me and then dropped down beside me.

"I wish you wouldn't go back to school tomorrow," he muttered unhappily. "You should take the rest of the week to recover."

"The doctor told me I could go back to a light routine starting tomorrow," I reminded him. "And I don't want to just lie around doing nothing. There are only a few weeks left of classes before I graduate. I don't want to mess that up."

"You're so fucking smart. It's not going to hurt anything if you miss a few more days," he grumbled. "Just tomorrow. Please. For me."

"Ugh," I complained, snuggling against him. "You know I can't say no when you say that."

I felt him smile as he kissed my temple. "Why do you think I use it so often?"

That made me snort. "At least you admit it."

"I'll have Mila tell the school you're taking one more day," he promised.

"Fine." My eyes were already feeling heavy. Being in a comfortable bed, with Mav's warmth seeping into me while he stroked his fingers through my hair, was more drugging than any pain medication. "But I'm going back Thursday for sure."

"Yes, ma'am." His lips skimmed over my cheek, but I didn't miss the way his lips felt as they lifted into a half smile. "I love you, River."

"Love you," I mumbled sleepily, before giving in and drifting off.

When I opened my eyes again, it was dark outside, and I was alone in bed. I still felt uncomfortable, but my stomach was now growling in hunger. Tossing back the blanket, I carefully climbed out of bed and padded into the living room.

The lights were off, but the television was on, and I saw Maverick sitting on the couch. The smell of pizza hit my nose, and my stomach snarled angrily. Coming up behind him, I wrapped my arms around Mav's neck and bent to kiss his cheek. One of his hands covered mine, his thumb rubbing over my wrist lovingly.

"How are you feeling, baby?"

"Lonely and hungry," I told him honestly, and he lifted his head to look at me.

"I'm sorry, babe. I didn't want to disturb you, but I should have come back after I made a few calls earlier." His voice was full of regret, and I moved around the side of the couch to climb onto his lap.

"You don't have to babysit me," I told him as I rested my head on his shoulder. "I'm just feeling a little...lost right now."

His strong arms contracted around me. "The doctor said you might feel a little fragile for a while. I'm sorry. Is there anything I can do to make it better?"

Tears stung my eyes, but I shook my head. "Just having you hold me helps," I whispered.

His lips brushed over my temple. "You said you're hungry?" I nodded. "I ordered your favorites. The pizza has pepperoni, sausage, green peppers, and green olives. There's honey barbecue wings, breadsticks, and I got that brownie-cookie thing you like."

Even though my stomach grumbled again, I only snuggled closer to him. "I'll eat in a minute. For the moment, I just want to sit right here and be sad a little longer."

He pressed his forehead to mine. "Take as long as you need. I'm not going anywhere."

TWELVE

RIVER

By noon the next day, I was tired of lying around doing nothing but feeling sorry for myself and longing for what I'd lost.

I'd promised Maverick I wouldn't go to school, but I hadn't said anything about work. While he snored away in our bed, I showered and got ready for the day. But when I grabbed my things to head out the door, I realized I had no way of getting to work on my own.

Dad hadn't dropped my car off yet like he'd said he would, and I wasn't going to go ask him for it. I had some savings, and I could put a down payment on a vehicle if I needed to. I didn't want anything from my father, especially if he was going to be an asshole about Maverick.

But he'd said he was going to let me have the car the day before. Muttering a curse under my breath, I grabbed my cell phone and realized I hadn't turned it back on. As soon as it lit up, I saw a text from my mom telling me to call her because she needed to talk to me ASAP.

Frowning, I hit connect without hesitating.

"Where are you?" she demanded, sounding out of breath.

"At Maverick's," I told her. "Kind of hard for me to go anywhere right now without a car."

"He still hasn't dropped it off?" she growled. "I'm going to kill him when I get home."

"It's fine," I tried to soothe. "I'll just buy my own car. I have savings, and the money Grandpa Hank put in my trust fund will be mine soon."

"You're keeping the car we bought for you," she argued. "Stop trying to be all adult and shut up for a second, little girl."

Her tone was full of sass, and I found myself fighting a grin. "Okay. What's up?"

"I think Delaney might have traveled up this way. I don't know if she's looking for me, or if she's just running scared from that motherfucker—" She broke off abruptly and inhaled sharply. "I've never wanted to put a bullet in someone more than this guy, River."

The quaver in her voice had me sitting up straighter. My mom wasn't a crier. I could count the times I'd seen her shed a tear on one hand with fingers to spare. That she was fighting tears now told me just how frayed her emotions were over the need to find her niece.

"It's going to be okay, Mom," I promised. "We'll find her."

"I told you I don't want you pulled into this. Tony is dangerous. He's already got men out looking for Delaney."

I rolled my eyes, thankful she couldn't see me. "Fine. You will find her. You and Aunt Raven," I amended.

"I know I'll find her. I just hope I can do so before Tony does." She blew out a frustrated sigh. "All right, enough of my pity party. Colt said you weren't feeling well. Is it that stomach bug going around?"

My hand automatically went to my belly. "Not really," I whispered, fighting the quaver in my own voice now.

The silence that filled my ear was loud as she tried to decipher what that meant. "Okay, little girl. I'm going to need more information than that," she muttered after a moment. "Did you have a bug or not?"

"Mom," I whispered, blinking back tears. "I..."

"River, baby, what's wrong?" she whispered back.

"I..." I clenched my eyes closed. "I had a miscarriage."

"Ah, honey. I'm so sorry." There was more than a quaver in her voice now. I heard her sniffling, and when she spoke again, her voice was just as choked as mine. "I...I had a miscarriage before we got pregnant with you, so I know you're hurting right now, my baby."

"I-I didn't know that."

"It's not something we talk about." I heard her blow her nose. "It took a lot out of me, and honestly, I wasn't sure I even wanted to try for another baby because I was scared. But you surprised me. It was the best surprise of my life, but afterward... I don't know, I guess I had a little PTSD, but I couldn't chance feeling that way again. So, we decided one kid was enough."

I'd never asked why I was an only child before, especially since my parents had always been all over each other. Now that I knew the reason, it made sense. Mom wasn't the type of person to let emotions rule her, but if she'd felt even half of what I was feeling right then, I knew it must have scared the hell out of her.

Knowing she'd gone through something like me and understood what it felt like, I found myself telling her everything that happened.

"Are you okay now, though?" she rushed to ask. "The bleeding, the pain?"

"I'm good, except this emptiness that I feel deep in my soul," I confessed.

"I know right now it might not seem like it, but it does get better," she promised. "It might take a while, but one day it will just be a dull ache and not the painful throb it is today."

"I hope so," I murmured. "I just want to keep myself busy so I don't have to constantly think about it. I was going to go into the shop and see if there's anything that needs to be done, but Mav is asleep and I don't have a car at the moment."

"I'll call your dad right now and make him bring it to you."

"Nah," I told her with a grimace. "I'll figure it out. I'll just call Mila."

"River, stop being so adult."

A soft laugh escaped me. "Mom, I hate to break it to you, but I *am* an adult now."

She huffed. "Shut up, little girl. I'm not old enough to have an adult daughter."

The pout in her voice only made me laugh more, and it felt...good. "Yeah, okay. I'm going to go now. Whatever you're doing, please be careful."

"I love you," she murmured softly. "Don't ever forget that, okay?"

The smile faded from my face as tears stung my eyes. "I-I won't." I swallowed hard. "I love you too."

After I hung up, I just sat there for a while, letting my tears spill over. I hated crying, but I couldn't seem to stop it from happening. Being sad was exhausting and made my entire body ache. It wasn't an emotion I'd had to experience all that often in the past, but it seemed to blanket me at that moment.

Once I had my emotions under control, I decided to call Kingston. Not only did he have a car that I knew he would let me borrow until I either got mine back or bought a new one, but he was my favorite male cousin. His mom and my dad were best friends, and Aunt Quinn and Mom had been roommates before they'd married two of the Hannigan brothers. Kingston was more like my brother than my cousin since the two of us were both only children.

"It's the ass-crack of dawn," Kingston grumbled when he picked up after it had rung several times.

"It's after noon," I informed him dryly.

"Really?" He sounded dazed, and then I heard him shifting around. "Fuck, it is." His groan sounded like he was in physical pain. "Shit. I should have been up over an hour ago to help at Aggie's. Mom is going to kill me."

"Um, before you go to be murdered, could you pick me up and drop me off at the shop?" I asked hopefully. "I'm kinda without a vehicle at the moment."

"What?" he yelled. "Why the hell don't you have a car?"

I squeezed the bridge of my nose as a headache began to pound behind my eyes. "Can we discuss that after you pick me up? I'm sure you want to get to the diner before Aunt Quinn comes looking for you."

He groaned again. "Yeah, okay. I'll be there in fifteen."

I was waiting outside when he pulled up, thankfully in his car and not on his motorcycle. I wasn't hurting, but I didn't think riding on the back of a bike would feel all that great to me. I climbed into the front passenger seat as soon as he came to a complete stop.

"Why don't you have a car?" he demanded as soon as we were out on the road.

I told him about Dad supposedly bringing mine over, but he hadn't, and I wasn't sure if he was going to. "I don't really care if he does," I told Kingston with a shrug. "He paid for it. Let him keep it. I'll get my own."

"I'm sure Aunt Kelli will have shit to say about that," he muttered unhappily. "He's being such a fucking prick over this whole thing, River. I knew he was going to be pissed about you and Maverick, but I figured he would get over it once he saw how much Mav loves you. This..." He tightened his hands around the steering wheel. "He needs a good knock upside of his hard head, if you ask me."

I wrapped my arms around myself, fighting off a chill. It wasn't even cold out, but I still found myself shivering. "I'm just glad no one got hurt at the party. My fear was that Dad would kill Maverick then and there. I call it a birthday miracle that no blood was shed."

"Yeah, I guess," he said with a grunt as he pulled into the parking lot of Aggie's. "You take the car. I'll catch a ride with Mom later. It's not like I need this damn thing right now anyway. I've got my bike, so you keep this as long as you need to."

Giving him a grateful smile, I leaned over and kissed his cheek. "Thank you," I murmured and was rewarded with him wrapping me in a tight hug.

"Happy belated birthday, by the way. Sorry I didn't get a chance to say it at the party." He pulled back and gently tapped me under my chin with his fist. "Don't drive fast. At least ten people will murder me if something happens to you in this thing."

I smacked another kiss on his cheek. "You know you're my favorite cousin, right?"

Opening his door, he winked at me. "Of course I am. I'm everyone's favorite."

Snickering, I climbed into the driver's seat. After adjusting everything, I pulled my seat belt on and drove the few miles to the Ink Shoppe.

It was still early, so no one else was there yet. The door was locked, so I used my key and opened the back door. Maverick said his mom had gone in the day before to help run the front for his dad, but she normally didn't do the things I took care of, like count inventory in the stock room and make sure the receipts were in order so I could keep up with the account books.

Locking the door behind me, I walked to the front of the shop and booted up the computer system. While that was getting started, I went into Uncle Spider's office to see if there was anything in there in need of immediate attention. Sometimes he left me notes in case he needed a certain ink ordered in time for a specific tattoo. Some colors of ink weren't kept in the shop because they weren't regularly used and it would be a waste, so we only ordered it if a client asked for it in advance.

As expected, there were a few things I needed to order, so I went into the stock room to see if we were low on anything else.

Opening the door, I was surprised to find the light on. Frowning, I took two steps into the room and froze when I saw the blanket Mav and I used to make a bed sometimes was lying on the floor. I kept it neatly folded up and hidden away, so I knew Uncle Spider or Aunt Willa hadn't messed with it.

"Someone's been in here," I muttered to myself. It wasn't the first time I'd thought that something was off in the storage room. The week before, when Lyric had come to pick up his package of ink, the box had been in a different location than I remembered placing it originally, and I thought there had been a smudge of what looked like blood on the box.

At the time, I'd just thought I'd moved it and hadn't remembered because I was so scatterbrained from being pregnant. But now, finding the blanket on the floor, having obviously been slept on, I was sure someone had been in the storage room.

I made sure to lock up every night, so I knew unless the person doing it was some kind of magician with a lockpick, then that wasn't how they were getting in. And other than a few misplaced things, along with the use of the blanket, nothing else had been off. There was no missing money, no missing supplies, and nothing had been vandalized.

My heart squeezed as I imagined someone breaking in just to keep warm and sleep. But as much as I felt sorry for whomever it was, I couldn't let it continue. I wouldn't risk anything happening to the shop just because I felt sad for a homeless person.

Muttering a curse, I walked around the shop, checking all the windows. It was in Maverick's room that I found where the person had been getting in. His window was closed but unlocked. Upon closer inspection, I saw the smudge of fingerprints. They were small, telling me the person had slender fingers, making me think it was either a kid or possibly a woman. Definitely not a man, because all the men I'd ever met had wider fingers than those prints would match.

My curiosity got the better of me, and I walked outside. Starting at Maverick's window, I looked around for any footprints and found a few sets several feet away. It had rained the day before, so the dirt was still slightly damp, making the footprints stand out. Bending, I took a picture of them with my phone. By the size and shape of them, I would have guessed it was a woman in running shoes.

Straightening, I kept my gaze on the ground and tried to follow the prints. When they led me to the woods, my stomach dropped. The thought of the girl—which was what I pictured now that I'd seen the footprints—sleeping in the woods with nothing to keep her warm at night broke my heart.

I ran back into the shop and grabbed the blanket then pulled a few bottles of water from the small fridge we kept in the front. I had a supply of snacks under my desk, and I selected a few bags of chips. None of the drinks or food had been touched, which bothered me even more.

Was the girl hungry? Thirsty? What was she eating if she wasn't eating my snacks, damn it?

Wrapping them in the blanket, I carried them out to the edge of the woods. I left everything out of sight of the shop so no one would ask questions, but where I hoped the girl would easily find it.

As I started back to the shop, I glanced over my shoulder one more time, hoping I might catch sight of someone. But I couldn't even sense anyone. Shoulders dropping, I entered through the back door and finally got to work.

THIRTEEN

MAVERICK

On my way to work, I stopped by Aggie's to grab some food, knowing River wouldn't have stopped to get some for herself. I wasn't happy she'd gone into the shop when she should have been resting, but it didn't surprise me.

My girl wasn't one to sit around doing nothing. She didn't like to keep still, and she always wanted to earn her own way. It was why she'd started paying her own car insurance when she first got a vehicle, even though her mom was insistent that she didn't need to worry about it.

Walking into the diner, I went straight to the counter where Aunt Quinn was taking care of to-go orders. Seeing me, she smiled and her eyes lit up. "Hey, sweetie. Kingston is working on your order right now."

"Thanks," I muttered, dropping my huge body onto one of the stools.

She grabbed a pot of coffee and a mug, pouring me a cup. "You look like you need this more than I do," she said with a shake of her blond head. "Are you doing okay?"

"I'm good," I assured her before swallowing half the contents of the mug in one gulp.

"Yo, man," Kingston greeted as he walked out of the kitchen with a bag full of to-go boxes. "I put in a few extra onion rings for River. She looked like she needed a little more meat on her bones when I picked her up this morning."

"Yeah, thanks for lending her your car," I told him, handing over my card to his mom to pay for the food. "If her dad doesn't bring hers back by tomorrow, I'm going to take her shopping for a new one. Maybe an SUV." I would feel better if she were in something as big as a tank and just as sturdy. Her car was safe and pretty strong, but I needed her in something bigger.

He shrugged. "Take your time. I don't need the cage anytime soon." He tossed in some packets of ketchup, ranch dressing, and a few other condiments he knew River liked.

As big and as inked up as Kingston was, he didn't look like he spent half his time behind a grill flipping burgers, but when he wasn't working at his dad's bar or on runs for the MC, the guy was a pretty badass cook. Aunt Quinn had been teaching him how to run Aggie's since he was old enough to wipe down a table.

"Call and set up a time for your new tattoo," I told him as I took the bag from him. "No charge."

"Dude, you ain't giving me free ink." He put his elbows on the counter and leaned forward. "The girl might as well be my baby sister the way I love her."

"I'm still not going to charge you for the new piece," I argued.

He smirked. "You drive a hard bargain, my man. I mean, if you insist and all."

Rolling my eyes at him, I scribbled my name across the

slip Aunt Quinn handed over and then bent to kiss her cheek. As I turned to leave, it was to find Colt walking through the door.

Spotting me, he clenched his jaw. "Where's my daughter?"

I gritted my back teeth, hating that the man seemed to detest the sight of me now, but it wasn't anything I didn't really expect. Colt Hannigan was a hard-ass, and I got that he was overprotective of his only daughter, but he needed to realize I'd been protecting her for almost as long as he had. I wasn't ever going to let anything hurt her.

Even if the one doing the hurting was her own father.

"She's at the shop," I told him. "I'm taking her something to eat, so unless you need something, I'd like to get it to her before it gets cold."

"Yeah, she's not answering my calls." He grunted something about her being stubborn like her mother under his breath before raising his voice again. "Tell her I'm getting her car checked over before I bring it to her. New tires, brakes, oil change, all the fluids topped off. Need to make sure it's safe for her to be driving it."

"If Max is working on her car, then he would have told you I got the oil changed last week. And he did a full inspection. Her brakes and tires were fine." I shifted the bag in my hand. "But, yeah, I'll tell her."

As I passed him and walked out the door, he followed. "What do you mean, you got the oil changed? Since when do you do shit like that?"

I didn't turn to face him, instead calling over my shoulder as I headed for my bike, "Since you gave her the car. I'm the one who has always gotten the oil changed as well as made sure the tires and brakes were in working order so that she was safe on the road."

Once a month, I took her car to the garage, and Max checked it over for me. I couldn't sleep at night unless I knew my girl was safe in all aspects, including driving the short distances from home to school to work and back again.

"Are you telling me every time I've asked if she'd gotten the oil changed, that was your doing?" I shrugged and slung one leg over my bike. Once I was seated and had the food stored away, I finally looked at him again. "Just how long have you been with my daughter without me knowing, Maverick?" he snarled.

I met his gaze without flinching. "I've always loved River. From the time she could crawl, I have protected her. And I'll spend the rest of my life doing both." He took a menacing step toward me, and I just sat there. If he wanted to take a swing at me, he was more than welcome. "I know you don't like the thought of me dating your daughter, but the truth is, I'm going to marry that girl as soon as I can get a ring on her finger."

"The fuck you are!" he roared and charged toward me.

"Colt, stop!"

I tensed at the sound of Uncle Bash's barked command. Colt stopped only a few feet from me, his chest rising and falling in heavy pants as he glared at me, but he didn't take another step toward me.

My honorary uncle, godfather, and MC prez stomped up behind his brother-in-law, his blue eyes blazing. "What the fuck are you doing?"

"This has nothing to do with you," he growled. "This is between me and this worthless piece of trash my daughter thinks she's dating."

His words cut me deep, but I didn't let him see that by so much as blinking.

"Worthless piece of trash," Uncle Bash repeated. "Up

until River's birthday party, you've practically praised this boy. How many times have you said he was a hard worker, had a good head on his shoulders? Fuck, brother, you even said he would make a good husband a while back. And now you're treating him like shit on the bottom of your shoe."

Those electric-blue eyes landed on me, and the hardness on his face eased. "River is a smart girl. I trust her judgment in people as much as I would my wife's. That she picked Maverick as her man doesn't surprise me. He will watch over her, protect her, provide for her, and treat her like a queen."

I had to swallow the knot of emotions that filled my throat at his words, but from the look on Colt's face, it was all going over his head.

"Listen to me, brother," Uncle Bash muttered, lowering his voice. "I know how hard it is to accept that your daughter has grown up. When Lexa started dating Ben, I nearly lost my mind. But I learned my lesson, and you should have learned something from what we went through, too. Get on board with who your little girl loves or risk losing her forever."

Colt's nostrils flared, and he spat on the ground at my feet. "Fuck your lessons, Bash," he gritted out before turning and walking back into the diner.

I watched him go as dread churned in my gut. I had a bad feeling where River's dad was concerned, and I didn't like it.

Uncle Bash blew out a harsh sigh and turned his gaze from the closing diner door back to me. "I'll try again after he's cooled down a little," he offered.

I shook my head. "Don't bother. He's not going to accept me being with River."

"It's not because you aren't good enough, Mav," my

uncle tried to assure me. "For some fathers, they just can't let go of their little girls. He wouldn't be able to accept anyone."

"I get it," I said as the dread in my gut churned a little harder. "I just don't want it to hurt River."

But I knew my real fear was that Colt would try to tear us apart.

By closing time, I was so tired I could barely keep my eyes open, and even though I wouldn't say I was in pain, I was more than a little uncomfortable.

Fighting a yawn, I went through my normal routine to make sure everything was in order and ready to go for the next day before grabbing my things.

"Babe," I called out as I walked back to his room where he was finishing up the last of his appointments. He'd canceled the ones from the day before, and he'd had me squeeze some of them in between his clients for that day, so he was still working. "I'm on my way out. Do you need anything before I go?"

He lifted his gaze from the scripture he was doing on the older biker's back. "I'm good," he said as his gray eyes skimmed over me lovingly. "I'll finish locking up. Just be careful driving home, baby."

I crossed the few feet separating us and kissed him, glad that we didn't have to hide our relationship from anyone now. "Love you."

He grabbed my ass with one hand, giving it a squeeze

before reluctantly releasing me. "Love you, River. So fucking much."

I kissed the tip of his nose, told the biker goodnight, and then headed for the back door. As I headed for my cousin's car, I couldn't help glancing toward the woods. But like earlier, I didn't see any sign of anyone.

Back at the apartment, I took a shower and then climbed into bed. As I did, my gaze landed on the bottle of pain medication, but I quickly turned my back on it. Now that I was off my feet, my discomfort was mostly gone. Making sure my alarm was set for the next day so I could get to school on time, I snuggled under the covers and was asleep within seconds.

The feel of Maverick pulling me into his arms made me smile, and I snuggled closer before drifting back to sleep as he kissed the top of my head and whispered he loved me. When the alarm went off, I was so comfortable I debated taking another day off, but I was already three days behind on everything.

Carefully, I untangled myself from Maverick's hold and went into the bathroom to get ready. My mom had dropped off a box of my things at the shop the night before, and I found it in the living room where Maverick must have set it when he came in the night before.

My phone buzzed on my way out the door, and I looked down to find a text.

Nova: *Can you give me a ride home after school? I'm staying over to help tutor some of the high school kids.*

I shot her a reply, promising her I could. Nova was practically fluent in both Italian and Russian, but she had taken some of the other language classes the school offered. With our town so small, it wasn't all that much, but she seemed to enjoy American Sign Language and Spanish classes. She was only a seventh grader, still in middle school, but she was better than some of the teachers and had started tutoring several of the high school kids for extra cash.

As expected, I had a load of homework for each of my classes that I needed to get finished, as well as study for an exam I would have to make up on Monday. My backpack was straining at the seams as I crammed all my books into it at the end of the day. The damn thing was heavy, and I knew I shouldn't be lifting so much weight. The doctor had said I wasn't supposed to lift anything heavier than ten pounds, but my backpack was at least twenty.

Knowing Maverick would blow a gasket if he found out I wasn't following doctor's orders, I glanced around to see if Nova was ready to go. She knew where my locker was, and she normally met me there when I gave her rides. Which was at least once a week. Garett had his own car, but he was usually out the door as soon as the final bell rang. Sometimes before the last class even started.

The school was empty except for a few teachers who were packing up to go home, the custodian who was already sweeping the halls, and students who needed extra help. From the looks and sound of how deserted the place seemed, I was sure the kids Nova was tutoring were already gone.

Leaving my backpack on the floor, I closed my locker and started for the library where Nova usually tutored. Most of them had study hall the last period, and Nova got extra credit in her language classes for helping. With the middle school right across the road from the high school, she didn't have to walk far, and all the teachers trusted her, so they didn't try to micromanage her.

The library was on the other side of the building from

the senior lockers, so it was a bit of a walk before I reached it. Pulling out my phone, I texted Maverick to let him know I might be late opening the shop as I pushed open the door to the library.

Just as I hit send, I heard a crash that was so loud it startled me, and I dropped my phone. Cursing, I bent to pick it up even as I glanced around to see where the noise came from.

My mouth fell open as I stared at the mess that had once been the library.

There were bookshelves turned over, papers still in the air as they floated slowly toward the ground. Tables were overturned and broken chairs scattered around. But it was the two guys lying on the floor, both of them bleeding out onto the worn, decades-old carpet that had me gulping in fear. One of them had a knife sticking out of the side of his neck, while the other was lying at an angle that didn't look humanly possible—unless he was dead.

Nova stood in the middle of it, her blond hair in a tangled mess around her face. Blood was splattered over her shirt and pouring down her arm, dripping into a small puddle at her feet. Her bottom lip was swollen and split, as if someone had hit her, and there were angry red marks on her throat and arms that looked like fingerprints. She was breathing heavily as she stared wide-eyed around at the mess.

"N-Nova?" I whispered her name as I slowly straightened, afraid of startling her. "Sweetie, are you...okay?"

Her green eyes jerked to mine, and her face paled. "I... Um... They attacked me."

My gaze fell on the two men lying lifelessly on the floor in their own blood. "I can see that. Did you...do this?" I don't know why I was still whispering, or why I'd just asked such a stupid question. How could my tiny baby cousin have taken on two grown men, let alone killed them? "Ah, fuck, Nova. Is there someone else in here?" I rushed to her, my instincts revving to protect her.

Her eyes skirted around the room wildly, as if she were looking for any other dangers. "No, I don't think so. It was just them." Her breathing was starting to even out. "I-I have to call Ryan. That..." She pointed to the guy with the knife sticking out of his neck. "That guy works for Matias Ramirez."

"Who?" I muttered, but she was already looking for her phone. When she spotted it, she walked over to pick it up, but as she turned it over, I saw the screen was cracked. "Forget about calling Ryan. We need to call Ben."

She shrugged, then winced. "Go ahead. I have to tell Ryan."

Frustrated with her, I quickly called Ben. He picked up on the third ring, sounding distracted. "Hey, River. I'm in a meeting with the mayor, honey. I'll call you back—"

"Ben!" I yelled when he started to hang up on me. "Nova was attacked at the high school. The library is turned upside down, and there are two men..." I glanced at them, still motionless, but it appeared the blood had finally stopped flooding out of them. "I, uh, think they might be dead."

"Shit," he muttered. "I'm on my way. Are you or Nova hurt?"

"I'm fine." I glanced over at Nova, who was trying to call her best friend without slicing her fingers open on the shattered screen of her phone. "Nova's arm is bleeding, and she's moving kind of slow, like she's in pain. I think she might be in shock."

"I'll be there in two minutes," he promised. "Stay together."

The phone went silent, and I focused back on my cousin. She'd finally gotten her phone to work, and she held it to her it away from her ear so she didn't cut herself on the destroyed screen. "H-Hey," she said. "Okay, so don't freak out..."

"What's wrong?" I heard Ryan demand. "Nova? Tell me!"

"So, um, I think Ramirez might be a little upset with you for some reason." She grimaced. She blinked a few times then looked down at her arm. "When did that happen?" she muttered to herself. "Shit, I think I need stitches."

"Nova!" Ryan roared. "Why do you need stitches?"

She was still examining her arm, not even seeming to hear him. I walked over to her and took the phone from her slack fingers. "Ryan?" I spoke softly into the phone, making sure to not let it touch my ear. By the looks of it, Nova was lucky to have even gotten a call through. I doubted I could make the speaker option work. "It's River."

"River," he exploded. "Is Nova okay? She's scaring me."

I wasn't sure how to answer that without freaking him out more than he already sounded. The times I'd been around him, he'd always been so cool and laid-back, but now he seemed...unstable. "Do you know a person named Mathias Ramirez?" I asked, hoping I could ease him into it.

"Yes," he gritted out. "Did he do something? Is he there? I'll kill him with my bare hands!"

"He's not here," I hurriedly assured him. "But two men attacked Nova..." I looked around at the mess. It looked like a hurricane had blown through the room. "Or they tried to. They're...well, the men are dead now."

There was a long silence on the other end of the phone. "Dead?"

"Yes," I confirmed. "Pretty sure, at least."

"But how is Nova? Is she hurt?" I could hear him breathing heavily. "Tell me, River. I need to know."

"She will probably need stitches. There's a large cut on her arm." I couldn't tell how deep it was from all the blood, but I could make out it was a long slice that went down her bicep. "She seems a little dazed too, but other than that, I think she's okay."

"I'm on my way. I'll be there as soon as I can." His voice sounded choked. "Please watch over her for me."

"I will," I promised just as I heard sirens in the distance. "Ben is here. I should go. Nova needs to get to the hospital."

"Right," he rasped. "Tell her..."

I reached out and stroked my free hand over Nova's hair. "I think she already knows," I murmured. "Don't worry. I've got her."

"Thank you," he breathed before the phone went silent.

Ben burst through the doors only a few moments later, followed by two of his deputies. All three of them had their guns drawn, but when they saw us, they quickly lowered them.

The sheriff rushed forward, his eyes taking in everything all at once. "Ambulance," he ordered the other two men. His eyes still glued to Nova and me, he bent and checked the pulse of the guy who didn't have a knife sticking from his neck. "And the medical examiner." Straightening, Ben crossed the remaining distance between us and carefully pulled Nova into his arms.

She blinked up at him a few times before focusing on his face. "Hi," she said in a small voice.

Cradling her head in one of his huge hands, he wrapped

the other around her and rocked her against him. "Thank Christ you're okay," he breathed.

She jerked back from him. "I'm getting blood all over you."

"Wouldn't be the first time one of you Hannigans got me covered in blood," he grumbled. Bending, he picked her up in his arms just as more sirens filled the air. "River, sweetheart, call Raven. Tell her to have Flick and Jet meet us at the hospital."

FIFTEEN

MAVERICK

I BURST INTO THE EMERGENCY ROOM THAT WAS already overflowing with my MC brothers and family, my eyes flying around in search of River.

I'd barely gotten her text that she might be late opening the shop before sirens had been flying past my apartment. Not two minutes later, more sirens had alerted me to an ambulance, but I hadn't thought much of it.

Not until River texted me ten minutes later that she was on her way to the hospital and not to worry. How the fuck was I supposed to not worry when she said shit like that? I'd broken the speed limit getting to the hospital, but there was no sign of her anywhere.

"Mav!" I turned at the sound of my sister's voice to see Mila standing by the nurses station. She took one look at me, saw how desperate I was, and gave me a nod. "She's in the back with Nova," she said, waving me toward the door that would take me back to the exam rooms.

The nurse she'd just been speaking to opened the door for me, and I sprinted down the hall until I saw Uncle Bash and Aunt Raven. They stood beside Ben, who was speaking to them in low tones. Behind them, my dad was standing in front of a triage door, his arms crossed over his chest, his face blank but his eyes wild.

He was who I ran to. Who I knew would tell me the truth. When his eyes landed on me, he dropped his arms and reached one out to grasp my shoulder, steadying me. "She's okay," he said in a low voice. "It was Nova who was attacked. River wasn't even touched."

"You're sure? She..." I scrubbed my hands through my hair, biting back the words that had nearly spilled out. She had only just lost our baby a few days before. She was still recovering. She could have been in pain and wouldn't have told anyone, because she wouldn't want them to worry about her.

"She's fine, son," he said, his hand squeezing my shoulder reassuringly. "I wouldn't lie to you."

I nodded, knowing he would always give it to me straight, no matter what. Taking a deep breath to try to calm my racing heart, I glanced at the door behind him. "Is Nova okay?"

He glanced at the door then over at Ben. "Doc is in there now. Her parents are with her, and so is River. It was that fucking Colombian rival of Vitucci's."

"They came after Nova to make a statement?"

He shrugged. "That's the way it looks."

"Fuck," I muttered and turned to stand beside him.

As I did, the ambulance bay doors opened, and River's parents came in. "Raven." Colt grabbed his sister's elbow, turning her to face him. "Where is she?"

She gave him a quick hug before stepping back. "She's fine, Colt. Nothing happened to River, I swear."

"Then why the fuck is she in the emergency room?" he demanded.

Raven glanced at Aunt Kelli, who lifted her brows in question. "Ramirez's men came for Nova. River was going to give Nova a ride home, but when she went to the library to see if she was ready, she found Nova had been attacked."

"Fuck," Colt exploded. "Is Nova okay?"

"Doc is with her now. She has a knife wound that needs stitching up, but we're waiting to know more once Doc is finished examining her."

"But nothing happened to River?" Aunt Kelli's gaze shot to mine. When I shook my head, she visibly relaxed.

But when she shifted her attention to me, so did Colt, and I could feel his rage before he even took a step.

"What the fuck were you doing when you should have been protecting my baby girl?" he bellowed.

I squared my shoulders, prepared to let him get it all out. I understood—fuck, I wanted to rage a little myself. My fear that something had happened to River still lingered, even though I knew she was safe behind the door I stood in front of. He barely took a handful of steps before both Raven and Aunt Kelli blocked his path.

"Why are you yelling at the boy?" Aunt Kelli demanded, pushing at her husband's chest. "She was at school, dumbass. He was on his way to work."

"He should have—"

"What?" she interrupted him. "Followed her around like a lost puppy while she went to classes?" He sputtered for a moment before growling something low that I couldn't hear. "Shut the fuck up, idiot." She stepped into his personal space. "I'm tired of your tantrums, Colt. She's a grown woman now. River loves him, and they're together. Pull your head out of your ass and be happy for them."

The door behind me opened, and I turned around at the same time Dad did. Jet stood there with a lethal look in his eyes, but his gaze moved past us to his youngest brother. "If all you're going to do is yell and scream, then you should just go the fuck home, Colt."

"How is Nova?" he asked instead, his anger turning into concern for his niece.

"Doc is about to stitch her up." He stepped aside and looked over his shoulder. "River, honey, you look exhausted. You should go home, or to work."

"I promised Ryan I would stay with Nova." Her soft voice came from inside the room, but I couldn't see her over Jet's shoulders.

His lips tilted up in a grim smile. "I think he will understand if I take over guard duty." He shifted, and I finally got to see my girl. She was leaning on the exam table beside her cousin, who was lying down with her injured arm stretched out while Doc and Flick bent over it.

My eyes ate up the sight of River. Her hair was disheveled, and her clothes were wrinkled. There were dark circles under her eyes and her cheeks were pale, but she looked as beautiful as ever to me. When she lifted her gaze from Nova, it locked with mine and she smiled.

"Hi," she mouthed.

"Hey," I said with a wink. "How about I take you home, beautiful?"

I could tell she wanted to go, but she glanced back at Nova as guilt filled her eyes.

Nova reached out with her free hand and squeezed River's arm. "Don't worry about me. I'll be okay. You should go to work."

Pressing her lips into a hard line, River finally nodded and bent to kiss her cousin's cheek. "Call me if you need anything."

"I will. Love you," Nova murmured softly. "Thanks for staying with me."

"Love you too," my girl said as they hugged. As she stepped out of the triage room, her eyes skirted over to her parents, and I felt her stiffen when she spotted her father. She reached for my hand, and I entwined our fingers. "I forgot my backpack at school. I need to get it so I can finish all my homework and study for a test I missed."

Ben walked over to us. "School will be closed tomorrow, but I'll have one of my deputies get your bag and drop it off to you."

She smiled up at him. "Thanks, Ben. It was by my locker."

"No problem, honey." He shifted his gaze to me. "She's had a rough day. Don't let her do too much this evening."

"I'm fine," River argued. "It's Nova who had a nightmare of a time."

I tucked her against me, pressing my lips to her forehead. "I'll make sure she takes it easy," I promised.

"I'll be here and then at Raven's," Dad told me. "Cancel all my appointments."

I nodded. "Keep me informed."

"Will do." He pulled River away from me to hug her. "Glad you're okay, honey." To me, he growled, "Be safe." What he meant was, *keep her safe*. But he didn't have to tell me that. I'd die before I let anything happen to River.

As we started for the exit, her dad stepped into our path, while Aunt Kelli and Raven muttered for him not to cause trouble.

"I want you to go home," Colt told her, a hard edge to his voice that warned River not to argue. "I'll be there as soon as I finish up here."

"I'm going to work," River informed him pointedly, the

same tone in her voice that was in his. "And then I'm going home. With Maverick. That's where I live now, Dad."

"Your home is with your mother and me."

She sighed heavily, her shoulders drooping. "I'm too tired to argue with you about this."

"Which is why you should get home and rest," he snapped.

"Look, you might still be my father, but you no longer have the right to tell me what to do. I'm eighteen now. That means I get to make my own decisions." She leaned into me, and I stroked my hand down her back, offering her my support. "And I choose Maverick. When you stop acting like a five-year-old who had his toy snatched away, give me a call. Maybe we can have dinner together as a family or something."

"You are *not*—"

Aunt Kelli cut off his harsh retort. "That sounds like a great plan," she said with a tight smile. "I'll call you later, sweetheart. Love you."

"Love you, Mom," she murmured with a sad smile then tugged me out the door.

SIXTEEN

RIVER

As soon as we were outside, Maverick pulled me into his arms and held me so tight it was nearly impossible to breathe for a moment. I felt him tremble and knew he was quickly losing control. Leaning back as much as I could when he was squeezing the oxygen from my lungs, I cupped both sides of his face.

"I'm really okay," I promised him. "I was scared when I found Nova in the library, but that passed as soon as Ben showed up."

His throat bobbed a few times as he tried to swallow, then he nodded and lowered his head to bury his face in my neck. "If anything happened to you..." he choked out.

I combed my fingers through his hair. "Shh, shh," I soothed. "Nothing happened. I'm right here."

We stood there for several long minutes, just holding each other. In his arms, I felt safe, loved, wanted. It was the only place I ever wanted to be.

"River," I heard someone call my name from behind me, and I reluctantly shifted my head until I spotted Mila walking my way with Monroe at her side. Behind Monroe, two of her husband's men followed, their eyes vigilant, their hands under jackets as if ready to pull a gun at any sign of danger.

The twins threw themselves against their brother and me, smothering me in the Masterson triplets hug that I would never get tired of. Maverick freed one of his arms to pull his sisters closer and kissed the tops of their heads before brushing his lips over mine.

"Where are you going?" Mila demanded after a minute of our group hug.

"Work," I said with a tiny shrug.

Her eyes filled with concern. "Let me give you a ride, then. You shouldn't be riding on a motorcycle after... Yeah."

I glanced up at Maverick, silently asking his permission.

"Yeah, baby. Go with Mil. I'll be right behind you."

"Actually, could you take me over to the school so I can pick up Kingston's car?" I asked. I doubted I could get into the school to get my backpack, but Ben had promised he would have someone drop it off for me. Still, I needed to get my cousin's car. I didn't like having to rely on other people to drive me around, and not having a way to or from places made me feel a little anxious for some reason. It always had.

"No problem." She linked her arm through mine, and the twins urged me toward Mila's huge SUV. "Mon, are you coming with us?"

As answer, she opened the back door and climbed inside. One of Gian's men got in with her, while the other guard walked over to the car they must have driven Monroe to the hospital in. Maverick opened the front passenger door and then picked me up, placing me in the seat before leaning in to kiss me.

"Didn't want you to have to climb in, baby," he murmured softly as he pulled back. "I'm going to be right behind you. Mila." He glanced across to where his sister was now seated in the driver's seat and pulling on her seat belt. "Drive carefully."

"Sure thing, Dad," she grumbled, sticking out her tongue at him.

I was glad when his lips twitched up in a half smile, and I pulled him back down for another kiss. "I love you. Please don't worry about me."

He stroked his thumb over my jaw. "I always worry about you," he muttered. "When I don't have eyes on you, all I can do is wonder if you're okay."

"Aww," Monroe gushed from the back seat.

"Look, Mon," Mila said with a sappy look in her gray eyes. "We trained him so well for our River."

"Fuck off," he growled at her. "And make sure you go the speed limit."

Once we were out on the road, with Maverick right behind us on his motorcycle, Monroe scooted to the middle of the back seat and leaned forward so she was practically in the front with us. "Tell the truth," she commanded. "How are you really feeling? Mila told me what happened Monday. Are you in any pain?"

"I'm fine," I told her honestly. "No actual pain. A little discomfort at times, but it's nothing I can't handle."

"Are you...bleeding?" she asked hesitantly.

I shrugged. "A little, but the doctor said I could deal with that for up to two weeks."

"Does this mean you can't...you know, have more babies?"

Biting my lip, I glanced out the side window. The thought of never getting to have Maverick's baby hurt.

Monroe touched my arm. "Hey, I'm sorry. I didn't mean to make you sad."

I covered her hand, blinking back my tears before turning to give her a small smile. "It's okay. I'm just a little emotional lately. The doctor said I could still get pregnant, but the chances are cut in half because I only have one fallopian tube now."

"That's a good thing, though, right?" She gave me a bright smile. "I mean, half the chance is still a chance."

"Yeah," I agreed. "I just..."

"What?" she and her twin asked in unison.

I swallowed roughly and glanced at the side mirror, watching Maverick on his bike behind us. "I'm scared it might happen again."

"Lyric's aunt Lana had something like that happen to her. He told me about it the other night, and how she and her husband decided they would just let fate determine how many kids they would have, if any." Mila said, reaching one hand across the console to take my hand as she drove. "And then she had five babies. He said they were always really open about being nervous during the first trimester. I guess the anxiety won't ever go away, but River, babe, you can't let fear hold you back. I mean, if you want a baby. If you don't, that's okay too."

"Yeah," her sister agreed. "If you and Mav decide not to have kids, Mil and I already have plenty for you and everyone else to spoil rotten. So, it's not like Mom and Daddy will be all growly about not having grandbabies and put pressure on you."

I laughed. "True."

"Speaking of parents and pressure..." Mila pulled into the high school student lot and parked behind Kingston's car. "We heard Uncle Colt shouting in the waiting room earlier."

I pressed my lips into a hard line. "Yeah, he's still being

difficult. But at least he isn't throwing punches or trying to kill Mav."

"True," she agreed. "I'm just worried he's going to try to break you two up."

I couldn't help snorting at that. I knew my dad would try to come between Maverick and me. But he would learn he was just wasting his time, because Mav was my forever, and nothing short of death was going to tear us apart. "He can try all he wants. Nothing will come between your brother and me. Ever." Leaning over, I kissed her cheek, then turned to hug Monroe. "Thanks for the ride. I'll call you both later."

"Take it easy," Monroe urged, her brows pinched together in concern. "You're still recovering."

"I can't just sit around with my feet propped up and expect to be waited on hand and foot," I told her with a roll of my eyes. "I need to keep busy. It helps."

"In that case," Mila said as she leaned forward and pulled something from her purse that was sitting at my feet. "Take a look at some of this inventory I want to include in the store."

I took the thick folder from her and slid it into my own purse. "I'll let you know. The less time I have to think about all the crap that has been going on lately, the better."

"Just don't burn yourself out," my best friend warned. "I need you around for at least the rest of my life. Don't make any of us have to live without you. Do you hear me?"

I kissed her cheek one more time before opening the door. "I hear you, sexy."

Closing the door behind me, I walked back to where Maverick was waiting on his motorcycle. "Are we going straight to work?" he asked when I reached him.

I gave him a quick kiss before stepping back. "I don't

want things to pile up. And you need to take care of your clients. Slacker."

He grabbed me by the hips before I could get too far away and pulled me back. "Babe, if there was a choice between you and doing ink, it would always be you." His kiss was a gentle caress of his lips over mine, making my head swim as I sank against his chest and kissed him back.

Lifting his head, he tapped me playfully on the ass. "Go on. I'll be right behind you."

I blinked up at him, trying to get my brain to clear. "I love you."

"I know, baby." He traced his thumb over my bottom lip. "I love you."

Everyone was tense when Uncle Bash called church the next morning. I arrived at the clubhouse barely half an hour after I'd gotten the text from him, the parking lot already overflowing with the others' bikes. After what happened the day before, I knew our security level was red, and I wouldn't have been surprised if my uncle announced we were going on lockdown for a while.

Pocketing my keys, I walked into the building behind my fellow MC brothers. The others were already sitting in the common room where there were couches, chairs, and pool tables, and several televisions were mounted on the walls. I'd grown up in this clubhouse. It was a second home to me. Hell, I might have spent more time playing there than I had at my parents' house over the years.

"Mav, over here," Kingston called, and I moved through the still-growing crowd of brothers to where he was standing with Jack and Elias.

"How's River?" the three of them asked, almost in unison.

"She's fine. I left her sleeping at home since there was no school today." I would have rather brought her with me, or at least dropped her off at Uncle Bash's house so she wouldn't be left alone, but she'd whined and pouted when I'd tried to wake her up. Unable to leave without knowing she was protected, I'd set my Glock on the bedside table and made her promise to use it if she needed to. Gun safety was something every kid in our family learned at an early age, so I knew she could and would use it without hesitation.

But knowing Ramirez was out there, trying to take out someone I cared about and didn't care who got caught in the cross fire, made me anxious to get back to River.

Max walked over to us, his dark hair falling over his forehead as he eyed me hard. "How's my cousin?"

"Good, man. Tired but good."

He gave a nod, but he seemed distracted as his eyes scanned around the room. "Ryan arrived last night. He's still here, along with his mom and about twenty guards."

"Fuck," we all grumbled.

The MC worked for the Vitucci family, doing protection runs from the West Coast all the way to New York. Drugs. Guns. Even willing women at times. They had strip clubs all over the States, and sometimes they had girls who wanted—or needed—a change of scenery for whatever reason. Vitucci wanted to make sure each girl was relocated safely.

But just because we worked for them from time to time didn't make them our boss. We had our own work that needed our attention without having to babysit them when they came to visit.

"He wants to leave five of them here to watch over Nova," Max informed us, his jaw clenching. "Like we can't take care of one of our own."

"Now that we know there's someone after Nova, we won't let her go anywhere unprotected," Jack told him. "We can work in shifts. Take her to school, stay with her all day if we have to, and then drop her off at home. Whatever it takes, man. She will be safe."

I nodded along with the others. No one was going to touch Nova as long as we were breathing.

Uncle Bash, Uncle Hawk, and my dad came out of the office at the top of the stairs, causing everyone to grow quiet as our prez, vice president, and the enforcer joined us. On the bottom step, Uncle Bash lifted his hands.

"We all know what happened yesterday." Everyone nodded or grumbled, a few of the brothers muttering curses. "The mayor and the sheriff canceled school for the day while they plan to make the school safer. Ben's going to put a deputy at each school, but there aren't enough cops. I say we give them a hand. Starting Monday morning, we're going to be taking shifts. I want no fewer than two brothers at each school's entrances. Also, someone needs to be with the teachers who are doing bus and parent drop-off duties. After all the kids are safely inside, there will be a brother at each entrance to the school, so we know who is coming and going during the day. And then when the final bell rings, we'll have two at each entrance and one helping with bus duty as well as parent pickup."

There were a few complaints, but mostly everyone was in agreement with our prez's plan. Plenty of my fellow brothers had kids who went to public school, so they wanted to ensure their safety. Nova might have been the target, but that put anyone who was in close contact with her in direct danger as well.

"We will be coordinating with Ben and Raven on this, so expect a text with your schedule and which school you will be stationed at. Each and every one of us will be taking a shift, so if your scheduled time interferes with work or another obligation, let our queen know, and she will switch you for a time that does work."

He broke everything down for another fifteen minutes, answering questions as they were thrown at him. Once that was dealt with, he brought up whose turn it was to go on the next run and then ended church.

While the others didn't wait around and headed for the door, I pushed through the crowd to get to the prez. "Uncle Bash," I called out. He lifted his head as I reached him and my father. "I'm going to be at the high school with River, so tell Aunt Raven she can schedule me for every day. Morning and afternoon shifts. I don't care."

He nodded. "We figured you would want to, Mav, but I'll remind Raven."

"How is Nova?" I asked him.

He grimaced. "Her arm is hurting her today, but she hasn't complained about it because Ryan is at the house with her. But she can't hide the pain in her eyes."

"Does she need anything? I'll bring it over with River," I offered, knowing my girl would want to stop by and check on her cousin in person.

"I don't think so, but call Raven and see if she needs anything before you stop by." His gaze landed on something behind me, and his eyes darkened.

Turning my head, I found Colt standing a few yards away, glaring at me. I already knew his dislike of me was most likely permanent now, so I decided to ignore the hate in his eyes and shifted my gaze back to my uncle. "If you don't need me to do anything, I'm going to pick up my girl and drop by your house before we go to work."

"Yeah, kid. See you later."

Dad slapped me on the back. "I'll be at the shop later. River doesn't have to cancel my appointments for the day."

"I'll let her know," I assured him before heading for the exit.

River was sitting on the couch when I walked through the door drinking a cup of coffee. Her eyes were barely open as she sipped from the mug, her hair a sexy, tangled mess around her shoulders and her clothes rumpled from sleep. I stopped midstep after closing the door, entranced by just how beautiful she was and how fucking lucky I was that she was mine.

"Is everything okay?" she asked, her eyes opening a little wider when she saw me just standing there, looking down at her.

I nodded. "Just a quick session of church. Nothing too serious. We're going to be helping with security at all three of the schools for the next few weeks."

"Ah, so my man will be going to school with me every day?" she gave me a sexy little smirk. "I kind of like that."

I crossed to her and bent to kiss her quickly. "I thought we would drop by and check on Nova before going to work if you feel up to it."

She nodded. "Yeah, I want to see her. Let me grab a shower, and we can go."

While she was in the bathroom, I called Aunt Raven to let her know we were going to come over. Not wanting to be away from River any more than I absolutely had to, I drove Kingston's car since my bike wasn't comfortable for her at the moment.

Pulling into my uncle's driveway, I saw a handful of men in suits outside on the porch, with others stationed around the property, their eyes scanning the area as if the place was going to be invaded at any moment.

Once we were parked, I saw a sign in the yard of the neighbor across the street. "Hey, when did that house go on the market?"

River followed my gaze. "I'm not sure. I can't remember that sign being there recently."

"Do you want to take a look at it? If you like it, we could put in an offer..." The look on her face had my voice trailing off. "What?"

"Nothing," she muttered, ducking her head as she moved to open her door.

I grabbed her arm and tugged her around to face me again. "It's not nothing, babe. Tell me what's wrong."

"I just..." She sighed and shook her head. "I kind of like the house a few blocks over. But it's been on the market forever. I heard it needs so much done to it that it is basically a money pit, but... Ugh, I don't know. I really do like it. And I thought with a little time and TLC, we could make it our own."

"Okay."

Her brows pinched together. "Okay, what?"

Leaning over the console that separated us, I cupped her face in both of my hands. "Okay, we'll buy it. We'll put in the TLC it needs. We will do whatever makes you happy."

Her chin wobbled. "But it's so much work. I know you're busy. A house that doesn't need work will be easier."

"Easier doesn't mean better," I said as I brushed her lips with my own. "Call the real estate agent later, and set up a time for us to view the house. Then we can make an offer."

Her teeth sank into her bottom lip for a moment. "Really?"

"Yeah, really. Whatever we can't do ourselves, Reid can take care of for us." I kissed her again before finally pulling back. "It might take us a while to get everything the way we want them, but it will be worth it if you're happy."

"I think we should put the baby items over there," Mila suggested as we stood in the middle of our store. Elias stood between us, making notes because we wanted a few changes made, but before we could implement them, we needed to decide how to section off everything. "But we want to catch the eye of the college girls on their way to class, so I think all the designer items should be right in front of the window over here."

I nodded my agreement. "And then back here—" I motioned to the back section of the store "—we need a half wall so that the more intimate items can be viewed with discretion."

"Definitely!"

Elias made a few more notes on his iPad. "Reid can draw you up some possible layout ideas, and we can get together one day this week to discuss them. Mom will have the prices listed for each one, so you won't have any hidden surprises."

"Great," Mila said with a beaming smile for him.

I walked over to the huge front window. "Do you think

we should have a sign above the building, or have it painted across this glass?" I frowned, trying to picture a few different designs that might work.

"We can build you a sign, no problem. But if you want the glass painted, I suggest getting an artist," Elias said as he took a few measurements with an app on his phone before plugging them into his notes on the iPad. "We have a few we use for other commercial clients. I'll get you their information, and you can compare prices."

"Perfect," Mila said as she linked her arm through mine. "You're the best, Elias."

He gave her a wink. "Don't worry. I won't tell your man you said that."

"Tell him what?" Lyric growled as he opened the front door.

I snickered and moved across the room to grab my friend's arm, guiding him toward the back storage room. "Let's talk about shelf space for our extra supplies. Also, could we turn a small corner of the front into a private nursing area? Just big enough to fit a few comfortable chairs, with room to move around as well."

"Well, we could add another half wall, or you could just get creative with inventory and seclude a corner off in the baby section," he suggested as we stepped into the storage room.

"Good idea," I muttered, shutting the door. As soon as it was closed, I pulled him over to the back exit. "Remember that IOU that we discussed you giving me for my birthday?"

His brows lifted. "You have a dead body you need me to get rid of?"

"No, dummy," I said with a roll of my eyes. "This doesn't involve a corpse."

He crossed his arms over his chest, lifting his dark brows. "I'm listening."

"I want you to keep an eye on my dad."

"Okay, before I say yes or no to this, I'm going to need more details here, River." I could see the reluctance on his face already. I was asking him to spy on one of his fellow MC brothers. It went against everything he'd been taught about the brotherhood of being a part of the MC.

Which was why I knew I would have to cash in my IOU he'd promised me.

"You know that saying 'No news is good news'?" He nodded, and I let out a small huff. "Well, that doesn't apply to this situation. My dad has been too quiet over the past few days. Colt Hannigan and quiet are a scary combination. There has been no snarling or growling or threatening. He's waiting until my guard is down. Or worse, when Maverick's guard is down."

Elias gave me a hard look. "Or he's just accepting that you and Mav are together."

"Yeah, it could totally be that." I snorted, rolling my eyes again. "Get real. He's plotting something, Elias. And I need to be prepared for whatever he's going to throw our way." Still, he just stood there, looking reluctant. "El, please. I know this is asking a lot, but he could be planning to hurt Maverick."

"River, if you needed me to bury a body—or fuck, kill someone and then bury the body—I'd be saying yes in a heartbeat. No questions asked. But Colt is my brother."

"So is Maverick!" I cried, my frustration making my voice rise and tears sting my eyes. "I'm not asking you to kill my dad, damn it. Or even hurt him in any way. I'm simply asking you to keep tabs on him and let me know if he does something that could potentially hurt the man I love."

He muttered a curse, then groaned, long and loud. "Fine," he finally gave in. "But that's it. And only for a little while."

Relief made me breathless for a moment, and I nodded emphatically. "Yes, of course. I won't ask anything else of you. Thank you, Elias."

"Don't thank me," he grumbled unhappily as he opened the back door and stepped outside. "I feel like a fucking traitor for even agreeing to this shit."

"But you're not," I called after him. "You're being a hero."

"You are a pain the ass, River!" he yelled as he put his iPad into the saddlebag on the side of his motorcycle, then climbed on.

"True. But you love me anyway."

His eyes narrowed on me. "That's debatable right now."

"Ah, don't be like that." I leaned back against the side of the store. "Keep me posted."

"Yeah, yeah, yeah," he muttered, starting his bike.

I watched him ride away, knowing his grumpiness wouldn't last long. He just needed to pout and grumble about it for a few days, but he wouldn't let me down. Shaking my head, I walked back into the front of the store.

"Um, hello!" I squeaked when I found Lyric pressing Mila up against the wall, causing my best friend to giggle. "Could you two not work on more babies in the middle of our store, please? I know we are going to be selling all kinds of stuff just for mommies, but homemade porn isn't on the inventory list. Even if Lyric is lickable, I didn't take you for one to share the view, Mil."

"I know my man only gets hard for me, so I don't care who sees us," she said as she unwrapped her legs from around Lyric's waist. "And we're not working on more babies. Unless he wants to be the one waddling around for nine months. Then I'd be okay with that." Her face contorted with pain. "I hurt just remembering how badly I tore pushing out Isaac and Ian. That episiotomy scar goes all the way to my asshole."

"But you were a warrior, baby," Lyric soothed. "Not a single drop of drugs the entire time. You were a champ. And if we have a daughter, I doubt she would be nearly as large as our beasts."

"You've wanted a girl so flipping bad ever since you saw Gian with Gianna and Lillianna. And now Luca has little bitty Remi." She met my gaze and grinned. "Someone wants a little princess of his own to spoil."

He gave a shrug. "Yeah, I'm not going to deny it. I want a little girl who looks like her momma, just like my brother."

"But you have two sons who look just like you," she reminded him, exasperated. "I think that's enough for a few years, babe."

"Fine. We can wait for a few years. I guess. But if Luca and Vi have another girl before then, we're going to be doing some serious baby-making of our own, woman."

"Deal," she contended. "Now, quit your pouting and go to work."

I found myself snickering at the two of them as I grabbed my purse. "I need to head to work myself. Uncle Spider and Mav both have back-to-back appointments all evening, and I have a lot of inventory that needs to be put away today."

"Speaking of inventory," Mila said as she followed me out the door toward my car. Dad had finally dropped it off to me a few days before, but he hadn't stuck around once he'd handed over the keys. "Lyric knows a designer who wants to sell her clothes in our shop. I met her at the

Armstrongs' Christmas Eve party back in December, and she emailed me last night after Layla mentioned our store to her. Riley sent me a crap-ton of pictures of her latest designs, and I freaking love them all. I'm going to forward them to you in hopes of narrowing down the items. We don't have enough room for all of her things if we're doing baby stuff too, but several of her items could even go in our intimates section."

"Yeah, sure. I'll look at them tonight before I go to bed," I promised her as I opened the driver's door. Before I climbed in, though, I paused and then threw my arms around her neck. "Love you, Mila."

Her arms went around me, holding me tight for a moment. "Are you okay?" she whispered.

I pulled back with a tiny smile. "It gets a little better every day. I'm still sad, but my heart doesn't feel as heavy." My smile disappeared. "Is that a bad thing? Shouldn't I still feel lost?"

"No, girl. It's not a bad thing. It just means my brother has been doing his job taking care of you." She gave me another tight hug before stepping back. "I'll forward you the email from Riley."

There were already two other vehicles in the Ink Shoppe's parking lot when I got to work. Uncle Spider and Maverick had both been coming in early to take care of all the clients they'd had to reschedule recently. As I parked, my gaze went to the woods in the distance, and I wondered how my homeless person was doing.

I'd taken a few more bottles of water and some snacks to the same spot I'd left the blanket the past couple of nights. After the first night, the things I'd left had disappeared, but the past two nights, they were still there when I went to take more. I didn't know if the homeless person had moved on, or if maybe something had happened to them.

Trying to feel optimistic and hoping that my person had moved on, maybe to better and brighter things, I walked into the shop and got to work.

I could hear voices from both Uncle Spider's and Maverick's rooms. The sound of their tattoo guns was a steady beat in the background over the music as I counted the inventory in the stock room.

"Hey, babe," Maverick called, then appeared in the doorway. I glanced up from where I was bent over to find his eyes zeroed in on my ass. He licked his lips hungrily before rubbing his giant hands over his face. There was no hiding the thickness in his jeans, and the sight of how much I affected him melted me.

He'd been so patient with me, never once complaining that we couldn't have sex. Hell, it hadn't even been mentioned. But every morning, I woke up to his cock pulsing against me. His need for me was in every skim of his fingertips, every caress of his eyes.

We still had a little while longer to go before it was safe to have sex again, but I was counting the days until we could, just as much as he probably was.

He dropped his hands, and he adjusted himself before clearing his throat. "I can't even remember why I came in here," he grumbled to himself.

I laughed, a full-on belly laugh, for the first time since the miscarriage.

"Fuck, that's a pretty sound," he said, his eyes brightening as he watched me. "I've missed it."

Straightening, I crossed to him and hugged his waist. One of his hands cupped the back of my head, cradling me against his massive chest. "Are you hungry? I was going to go pick up some dinner."

"Yes, I'm hungry. But I don't want you to leave." He kissed the top of my head then stepped back. "That's what I came to tell you. There have apparently been some unusual break-ins lately. Nothing has been stolen or anything, but Ben has been getting some strange calls."

"Break-ins?" Instantly, my mind went to my homeless person.

"Yeah. Really weird shit. People saying they thought someone had been in their place. Random things misplaced, but nothing seems to be missing. Ben said one guy thought it was a ghost." He laughed, shaking his head. "It's probably just a few kids playing around. But I'd rather be safe than sorry. I don't want you here alone until it gets figured out."

I bit my lip, knowing he was about to blow up, but if other people were experiencing the same thing, I needed to speak up. "Mav..."

"What?" he asked, his gray eyes narrowing on me.

"There were a few times when things were supposedly misplaced in here over the last few weeks. Then one day, I came in and found our blanket on the floor." I pointed to where I'd found it. "Nothing ever went missing, but it just felt like something was off. When I found the blanket like that, I knew someone had been sneaking in and sleeping here."

"Fuck, baby. You should have told me," he growled, his eyes looking wild all of a sudden. "Someone was here, and they could have hurt you."

"I don't think she would have," I rushed to assure him. "I think she was just cold at night. Plus, there are coyotes out in those woods."

"She?"

I shrugged. "I think it's a girl. Maybe a woman. I'm not sure. But the finger and shoe prints I saw make me think it is."

"Fuck," he muttered. "How the hell did she even get in here?"

"You left your window unlocked."

"What?" he yelled, stabbing his fingers through his hair. "I left it unlocked... Motherfuck, I put you in danger."

"Stop, please. You didn't put me in any danger. It was just a homeless girl looking for a place to sleep safely." My heart hurt just thinking about her. Then I remembered my cousin Delaney, out there somewhere, and tears stung my eyes. "I locked the window and took the blanket out to the woods so she would at least have something to keep her warm. Sh-she must have been trying to find somewhere else to take shelter at night."

Maverick's arms wrapped around me, and I pressed my face into his chest as a sob snuck up on me. "Baby, don't cry," he pleaded. "I didn't mean to yell. I'm sorry."

"I just...I feel so bad...for her. I know I couldn't let her sleep here anymore, but I wish I could have done more." My tears soaked into his T-shirt. "She's probably all alone and scared. She might not have anyone who even cares about her. But I care. I don't want h-her to get into trouble."

He cupped the sides of my face and bent his knees until we were eye level. "I'll fix this," he vowed. "We'll find this girl and make sure she's okay. Maybe Jack's mom can let her stay at the women's shelter."

My heart lifted. "Really?"

He wiped away my tears with his thumbs, his eyes tormented. "Yeah. Just let me make a few calls. We'll get this taken care of. I promise."

I was so relieved, but my tears only fell faster. "Y-you're the best," I sobbed. "I-I don't deserve you."

"Ah, fuck, River," he groaned, tucking me against him again. "Don't say shit like that, baby. I'm the one who doesn't deserve you."

NINETEEN

MAVERICK

How hard could it be to find one homeless girl in Creswell Springs? Especially when the residents were already spooked at the thought that someone was breaking in to random businesses.

A fucking lot harder than anyone would think.

This girl really was like a ghost. In a town as small as ours, a new face would stick out big-time. Yet no one had seen her. Ben put the word out that he was looking for the girl, but since no one knew what she looked like, everyone was just looking for anyone they didn't recognize. After I told Dad about what River said, he'd called Uncle Bash and had all the brothers keep their eyes open for a sign of anyone new as well.

Hell, we weren't even sure if this was a girl or not. It could have been a little boy if we were going off the finger-prints and shoe size from the picture River had taken of the footprints outside of the shop. But I trusted my girl's instincts, so if she thought this was a girl or a woman, I would assume it as well.

It was driving me crazy that we hadn't found her yet,

because it was worrying River. And I hated when she was upset. She'd just started to get better after the miscarriage, and now she was all lost again over some girl she had never even set eyes on before.

"You okay over there, brother?" Kingston asked as we sat outside the high school entrance a few minutes before the last bell was supposed to ring. "You're looking a little murderous."

I blinked at my friend and MC brother, shaking away the thoughts of how down River had been that morning. "Yeah, man. Just worried about River."

He grimaced but nodded. "Yeah, I noticed she hasn't been herself lately. What with her graduating this weekend and her and Mila getting the store ready for the grand opening next month, I thought that she would be bouncing around with excitement. But when I took her lunch yesterday and ate with her in the cafeteria, she was all kinds of spacey and moody. Fuck, man, I thought for a minute she was going to cry, and I didn't know what to do."

Kingston had a helpless look on his face as he remembered, and I knew exactly how he felt. I experienced that emotion at least once a day when it came to my girl. Not being able to fix something for her—especially when I'd promised I would—was driving me insane. I was failing her.

The bell rang, and the school buses started up on one side of the school, while the drivers in the parent pickup line started their cars just as students started coming out of the exits. The majority of the high school students drove or rode with friends, so there weren't nearly as many pickups as there were at the other schools, which meant traffic wasn't as bad as it would be across the street where the middle school was.

With only this week left for the seniors, and the

following week the last one for all the other students before the summer break, everyone was starting to calm down a little for the first time since Ramirez had sent men to attack Nova. But I couldn't relax until River and Nova were safely at home each day.

"There's Nova," Kingston said as he watched his cousin climb onto the back of her dad's bike. Her blond hair was pulled back into a simple ponytail, and she had her back-pack slung over her shoulders. It took her a moment to get comfortable before she hugged her father's waist and he merged into the line of traffic to leave the school property.

As Uncle Jet pulled onto the highway, she waved at us. Kingston blew her a kiss, and I waved back before returning my gaze to the exit River normally came out of. I'd dropped her off that morning instead of letting her drive herself. She hadn't been getting much sleep lately, and I didn't like her behind the wheel when she was sleep-deprived.

Between graduation, working at the shop and the store to get it ready, as well as worrying about the homeless person and still healing from her miscarriage and surgery, my girl was going nothing but fumes lately. But she couldn't seem to turn off her brain at night to get some sleep. I was thinking about taking a week or two off from work so we could go on a vacation. Get her away from all the shit going on around us and making her soak up some sun down in Mexico.

It would be good for her.

And if we happened to come home married...

Well, then her dad would just have to suck it up and accept our relationship once and for all. He sure as fuck hadn't accepted that we were dating. When I saw him at the clubhouse or at MC events, all he did was glare at me. If I tried to speak to him, all I got was cold silence. River spoke to him on the phone once or twice a week, but she'd been avoiding his calls more and more lately because he acted more and more like a dick every time they talked.

She'd have to see him on Saturday at her graduation, and I thought that was why she was dreading it so much.

Finally, the door opened, and River walked out with just her purse in her hand. As soon as she was close enough, I reached out and grabbed her hip with one hand, pulling her up against me and kissing her. She made a little mewling noise deep in her throat, kissing me back. She had a doctor's appointment the next day, her second follow-up since her surgery, and I was praying we got the green light for sex.

But if we didn't and she needed more time to heal, I would gladly suffer my aching blue balls until her doctor thought she was ready.

When I lifted my head, we were both struggling to breathe, and a tiny smile teased at her lips. "Hi," she murmured, looking up at me through her lashes. "Long time no see, handsome."

I stroked my thumb over her plump bottom lip. "You good?"

She lifted her shoulder in a half shrug. "Just tired."

"Hey, little cousin." Kingston drew her attention to him. "How was your last day of classes?"

"Boring," she told him with a twist of her lips. "This entire week was pointless if you ask me. But attendance was mandatory if we want to walk at graduation the day after tomorrow." She let me take her slight weight for a moment, as if she didn't have the energy to hold herself up. "I really don't even know why I want to walk."

"Because it will make your parents happy," Kingston told her. "It was the only reason I did it last year."

"Yeah," she muttered, her eyes darkening. "My parents."

I tipped her chin up with my index finger so I could kiss her again. This one was slower, less demanding, to take her mind off her dad and pull her out of her head. When I lifted my head, she looked up at me dazedly. "Hi," I said with a grin. "You ready to get out of here?"

"Definitely," she breathed, then cleared her throat. "I have to stop by the store. I need to make sure the new assistant we hired is helping Mila get the displays set up correctly."

"I can help with any heavy lifting," Kingston offered.

"You just want to check out the new hire," she said with a mock glare at her cousin.

"Guilty," he said with a smirk. "But I'm free labor. Can you really afford to turn that down right now, sweetheart?"

"You got me there," she grumbled. "Fine. I would really appreciate it. If you don't mind?"

"You know I'd do anything for you," he said with a wink.

As she climbed on behind me, I sent him a chin lift, thanking him for helping her. It also put me a little more at ease, knowing he would be at the store with her and Mila. Lyric was right next door, but if something were to happen, it could take my brother-in-law time to get to the girls should they need assistance in any way.

I'd been trying to stay with them when River went in right after school, but she knew my schedule too well and always made me go to work so I didn't have to cancel on one of my clients. With the local college having released the week before, I wouldn't be nearly as busy for the next few months after this weekend, which was why she didn't want me to piss off any of the clientele and lose business.

River put on the helmet I gave her then got comfortable. She pressed the front of her body against mine, her arms going around my waist and her hands settling right above the bulge in my jeans, causing me to groan at how good she felt against me. I covered her hands, stroking my thumbs over her petal-soft skin for a moment before starting my bike. I felt her press her face to the center of my back as we pulled onto the road in the direction of her store.

While I drove, her hands teased lower, torturing me. I was in agony by the time I pulled into the parking lot behind the building. When I helped her off, she had a mischievous look on her face, and that sight alone was worth the ache in my balls. I was just thankful she didn't have that haunted look in her eyes anymore.

Still holding her hand, I tugged her closer. "Be good. Don't work too hard. I have appointments all evening, but if you need me, call."

She took off her helmet and handed it to me. "I'll be over as soon as I take care of a few things here."

"Get Kingston to drive you home to get your car." I swatted her on her ass with my hand, causing her to mewl and press even closer against me. I dropped a kiss on her lips when she pouted up at me. "Soon, baby," I promised. "If we get the green light tomorrow…"

"Oh, we're going to get the green light." She touched her lips to my ear. "And then I'm going to ride you all night long."

"Christ, woman," I growled. "Go to work before I do something that might hurt you."

Her eyes brightened. "Is my man at his breaking point?"

"Getting closer by the second," I muttered, stealing another kiss. "I love you."

"Love you," she said as she stepped back reluctantly. "See you soon."

She walked inside just as Kingston pulled up beside me. "I'll keep her safe, man," he said as he fist-bumped me. "You know I'll protect that girl with my life."

At work, I spent the next few hours doing ink. But as the evening wore on and I didn't hear from River, I started getting anxious. She'd said she wasn't going to be at the store all that long, and it was already past dinnertime. Muttering a curse when I checked my phone and found no missed calls or texts from River, my sister, or even Kingston, I was starting to call my girl when my phone rang.

Seeing it was Colt, a feeling of dread made my heart drop into my stomach, and I picked up before it finished ringing the first time. "Yeah?"

"I think I found your homeless girl," he said in a cold tone.

"Where?" I was already grabbing my keys and heading out the back door without even telling my dad, who was still working on his own client.

"Motel out by the interstate. After the staff noticed some things off the last few days, Ben got a call, and I was at the station. Told him I would check it out. The front desk guy said they think she might be sleeping in Room 119. Said the bathroom has been broken, so they had it out of commission, and it would have been easy for her to use it without anyone knowing. If there hadn't been a few things going missing, they might not have noticed."

"I'm on my way," I told him as I swung my leg over my bike.

He didn't answer, just hung up. Telling myself I was just glad that I could follow through on my promise to River, I headed for the highway. There was only one motel by the interstate, and the place wasn't much to brag about. There were two different hotels in town that got steady business, but the motel was somewhere mostly used by truckers because it had a reputation for having a ready supply of hookers on call.

Not that Ben had ever been able to prove it. There was rarely any trouble from the place, so he didn't try to shut it down.

When I got to the motel, I didn't see Colt or his motorcycle. But I had the room number, so I parked right in front of 119 and headed inside. The door was unlocked, and I stepped into the darkened room, reaching for the light switch.

When nothing happened, I took a few steps inside and felt a sudden burning in my neck.

"The fuck?" I muttered, slapping at the spot where it felt like I'd been stung by a wasp. The burning feeling was spreading, and my entire body felt heavy. I blinked, then felt the world sway as complete darkness swallowed me whole.

TWENTY

RIVER

"I'm exhausted," Mila said with a yawn as we finished putting the last of our inventory on the racks.

Between Avery, who was our new hire, Mila, and me, we'd gotten everything done with Kingston's help doing the manual labor. I wiped the sweat off my brow and pulled my phone out of my back pocket, only to groan when I saw the time.

"Mav is probably worried," I muttered, calling him. It rang and rang, and I swallowed a sigh, knowing he was going to be upset with me for not calling him. We'd been so busy that time had gotten away from me, and I hadn't realized it had gotten so late. My plan had been to help out a little before going to the shop.

When my call went to voice mail, I figured he was just with a client, and I hurriedly told the others goodbye before running out the door with Kingston. He gave me a ride to the apartment, where I picked up my car, and I tried not to go over the speed limit on my way to the Ink Shoppe.

Pulling into the parking lot, I saw that Maverick's bike wasn't where it should have been. Frowning, I reached for the door, wondering if he'd gotten so worried, he'd gone looking for me. But I hadn't seen him on the road…

My phone rang just as I was stepping out of my car. Seeing who the caller was, I quickly answered. "Hey, Elias."

"You know the interstate motel?" he clipped out as a greeting.

I stopped with my hand still on the driver's door. "Uh, yeah?"

"Get there. Now. Room 119. I'll explain when you get here." I heard the ice in his voice and knew it was bad. Elias didn't do fire and ice; he was like a cuddly teddy bear. Until you pissed him off. Then he could get scary. The fire was for when he was about to beat the fuck out of someone. The ice…when he was trying to control the flames.

Without questioning him, I got back in my car and turned it in the direction of the interstate. But as I was driving, I got a text. Worried it was from Elias or Maverick, I picked up my phone from where I'd tossed it in the cupholder and glanced down at the screen really quick.

Only to do a double take.

"No," I whispered, my foot slamming on the brake.

The text was from a number I didn't recognize, but the picture was something I knew all too well. It was Maverick, completely naked, on a bed with two girls lying on either side of him. They were touching him, kissing his bare chest while one of them took the selfie.

I felt physically ill looking at the picture, but in my heart, I already knew it wasn't what it appeared. Maverick would never cheat on me. I knew it all the way down to my soul. It didn't matter that we hadn't had sex in weeks. He would have gone without it for years if I wasn't able to give it to him.

He loved me. Was loyal to me.

Yes, I might get jealous when he had a female client, but that wasn't because I thought he would cheat on me. I was just possessive and hated the thought of him having to touch someone other than me.

In the picture, his eyes were only slits, barely open. I couldn't even tell if he was even awake.

The longer I looked at it, the more and more pissed I got.

Tossing my phone into the passenger seat, I slammed my foot harder on the gas and left skid marks on the road as I blaze a trail in the direction of the run-down motel.

As soon as I pulled into the parking lot, I saw Elias standing by his bike, which was parked right beside Maverick's. I slammed on my brakes and shifted into park, but I left the car running as I jumped out.

"Is he okay?" I demanded, running toward Room 119.

Elias clenched his jaw. "What you're about to see isn't what it looks like. I want you to understand that."

I snorted. "I know that. Someone sent me a picture. Anonymously, of course." But the dread in my gut was already telling me I knew who was behind all this. That it was Elias who had called me there only further confirmed it.

Reaching the door, I pushed it open, not surprised it wasn't even locked. Inside, I found the two girls from the picture lying on either side of my naked man. They were both in only bras and panties, and they hadn't even pulled the sheet up over Maverick to cover his dick.

Their heads snapped up as I barged into the room, their faces losing all color as I marched straight to the closest one. In a rage, I grabbed her by the hair and jerked her off the bed. Her scream filled the room, and Elias watched from the open door in gaped-mouth amazement.

Slinging the girl away, I reached across Maverick for the other, but she yelped and made a run for it. However, Elias was blocking the only exit, making it all too easy for me to grab her from behind and toss her over to where her partner in crime was sobbing on the floor because I'd pulled a huge chunk of her hair from her scalp.

From the bed, Maverick groaned as if he were in physical pain. "Babe?" he slurred, and I knew—fucking knew—he'd been drugged. "What's all the...screaming 'bout?"

"Don't worry, baby," I murmured in a soothing voice, not wanting to worry him. "I'll take care of this. You just sleep it off."

"Love you, River," he groaned.

"I love you too, baby," I told him as I glared down at the two women huddled together on the floor.

"I've been following Uncle Colt like you asked," Elias said from the doorway. "I was going to say to hell with it because I thought for sure you were worried for no reason. Fucking glad I didn't listen to myself. Yesterday, he started acting shady, and I saw him come out here. He was in the registration office for over an hour, and then he went home. A few hours ago, he came back here and walked into this room. On his way out, I heard him talking to someone. I don't know why, but I stuck around, making sure I stayed out of sight. Maverick showed up not long after..." He nodded his head. "Never saw these two. But I heard him mutter something then a crash and these two cursing about him weighing so much. I waited a little bit to see what they might do, but I knew it must be a setup."

"I knew it was a setup as soon as I got the picture." I crouched down in front of the girls. "Colt Hannigan set this up, right?" They both nodded hurriedly. And my dad got exactly what he wanted to accomplish with this shit.

My heart broke.

It shattered, right there on the dirty floor of that disgusting motel room. Just as he'd hoped.

Only, he was the one to make it break. Not Maverick. Never ever Mav. He loved me too much to ever want to hurt me.

Dad was the one who killed a part of me then and there.

But I sure as fuck wasn't going to let him get away with it.

"How much did he pay you?"

"Two grand," the one who wasn't crying said with a gulp. "A thousand each. Cash. A-all he wanted was for us to drug this guy, get him naked, and take those pictures. Th-that's all, lady. We...we didn't mean any harm. It was just about the money. Ya know?"

I gave her a grin, but it only made her cower back against her friend. "Yeah, I do know." I straightened. "Get dressed. Your job isn't over. You two are going to be earning every penny of that blood money he gave you."

THURSDAY NIGHTS WERE CHURCH NIGHT. Always had been, for as long as I could remember.

It was just after nine when I pulled up outside Hannigans' and parked. Getting out, I shut the door calmly and walked into the bar like I owned it. Technically, I would own a percentage of it one day.

If I didn't burn the fucking thing down.

The idea was all too tempting, but my cousins loved this damn place, and I knew it was their future. As much as I hated my father right then, I couldn't take it away from them.

As soon as I walked through the door, the entire bar

went quiet, and all eyes turned to me. But mine zeroed in on Dad, and I walked toward him, keeping my expression neutral. He didn't even flinch when our gazes met, and somehow, the pain in my chest only intensified.

After everything else he'd done that day, I'd thought he couldn't hurt me more, but realizing he didn't feel an ounce of remorse killed yet another part of me.

"River?" Uncle Bash stood. "Honey, is everything okay?"

"I thought this MC was about brotherhood," I said, keeping my eyes on Dad. "I always loved that about this family. That it was so big, so loyal to one another. That even though I only had a few blood uncles, I had many, many more who were honorary. You all took care of one another. Protected one another."

"River..." Uncle Bash stepped in front of me, blocking my view of his brother-in-law. "We're in the middle of something. You shouldn't be here."

Slowly, I lifted my eyes to his face. "This is between my father and me."

"What is?"

"Uncle Bash, I know that his punishment should be to face the enforcer. And I would honestly love to see Uncle Spider kick Dad's ass right now." I licked my suddenly dry lips. "But I'm going to ask you to please let me have the honor of making him pay."

He grasped my shoulders. "You need to explain to me what's going on, River. Right now. I've seen this look in Raven's eyes one too many times, so I know you're out for blood. But I need to know why."

I tilted my head to the side, studying him for a moment. "What would happen if a brother did something that hurt another brother. Physically hurt him, I mean."

"He would face the enforcer," my uncle confirmed.

I nodded. "Exactly. And what would happen if, say, this brother didn't do the hurting himself, but paid someone else to do it?"

"Again, he would face Spider."

I'd known that when I decided to come here. Knew I was taking a huge chance in just asking, but I had to try. "Well, I'm asking you to let him face me instead."

Behind him, I heard a chair scrape across the floor as it was pushed back. "Step aside, Bash," he commanded. "Let her have her way."

My hands fisted at my sides, and after a hesitation, Uncle Bash released me, taking a few steps away.

"Well, here I am, River. Say what you want to say."

I just stood there, staring at the man who had raised me. He had given me life. He was the first man to love me... supposedly. But at this point, I wasn't so sure if he did. He had no idea what the real me was like. Had never really tried to find out. But this...what he'd done...this pain went much deeper than realizing he didn't know the little details about me that made up who I was.

It was agony. Worse than any pain I'd ever felt, and that included the physical pain of having my fallopian tube rupture. This pain hurt even more than losing my baby.

The man who was supposed to love me and protect me was the same man who had so effortlessly broken a part of me no one would ever be able to fix.

Was this what it felt like when Mom's own father had shot her?

The thought made me ill. I was comparing what my dad did to what my grandfather had done. It wasn't the same, but the betrayal felt like it was.

Hers had tried to kill her.

Mine...well, he might as well have ended my life, because the pain he'd left behind was soul-crushing.

If something had happened to Maverick, I would have died too. If I'd lost him, there would be nothing left for me. Not my family, not my friends. Nothing, because my world began and ended with that man.

I pulled the promise ring Maverick had given me all those years ago off my index finger and held it out in the palm of my hand. "Do you see this? Mav gave it to me when I was fifteen. It came with his promise that he would love me forever. That, no matter what, it was him and me. I told him I loved him for the first time that day. Made my own promises. There is nothing you could possibly say or do that would ever make me doubt that he loves me. That his loyalty is to me."

His eyes narrowed. "You two have been together since you were fifteen?"

"Longer," I spat the word at him, then shifted my gaze around the bar, taking in my uncles—both blood and honorary. "Tell the truth. Who here knew about Maverick and me before my birthday party?"

A few people started coughing, some of them dropping their gazes. Dad's eyes widened as I fought a grin. So many of them had known, but not one of them had said a word.

"I knew," Uncle Jet was the first to speak up.

"Me too," Uncle Hawk said with a shrug.

"I suspected," came from Uncle Raider.

Uncle Spider sighed heavily, pulling my eyes to where he sat in what everyone referred to as the Originals' booth. "I suspected, but I didn't know for sure. It was weird. Mav never flirted with anyone. Never even looked twice at any other female. But then he would get around you, River, and I could see he had feelings for you. I didn't think you two were together, but yeah, I knew he was in love with you."

I sucked my bottom lip between my teeth for a moment before swinging my gaze back to Dad. "It was the best-kept secret that half this fucking town knew about for years. Everyone knew about it but you, until my birthday. I begged all the people I was aware of who knew not to tell you, because I knew you would freak out and try to keep us apart. At my party, I shook the whole time, because I was scared you would kill him just for asking to be my boyfriend. When I blew out those candles on that ridiculous pink cake, I wished for *you* not to break my heart. Only...you did exactly that." My heart hurt just remembering, and I had to swallow the knot that tried to choke me before I could go on. "But tonight, you went beyond that, Dad. You didn't just break me. You shattered a part of me that I will never be able to put back together!"

"Why are you here, yelling at me?" he demanded, his nostrils flaring as his own anger grew. "He's the one who cheated on you."

I threw my head back and laughed out loud. It was a hilarious punch line that he didn't quite get. As he continued to glare down at me, my laughter abruptly dried up, and I looked up at him in disgust. "You're an idiot. A selfish, worthless idiot. I knew as soon as I got that picture that it was a setup."

"Honey, I'm sorry. But you should know that Maverick isn't worth your time." His green eyes filled with faux remorse, his voice almost cajoling, and I wanted to slap him. Instead, I replaced the ring on my finger and stepped back. "I know it hurt to see him with those girls, but I couldn't let him continue to lie to you. He's been seeing both of them for weeks, and I—"

"Stop lying to me!" I screamed, fed up with all of it. "I know everything, Dad." Doubt crossed his face, but it quickly cleared. Before he could speak, I whispered, "And so does Mom."

This time, his face paled.

"No," he quickly denied. "She's been so busy lately, she doesn't know anything. She's barely been home. How could she possibly know...?"

The sound of another vehicle pulling up outside the front door reached me, and I lifted my brow at my father. "That will be her. And the hookers you paid. Also, Aunt Raven and Aunt Quinn."

His throat bobbed as he looked over my head just as the door opened and Mom walked in. Aunt Quinn was right at her side, the two working girls behind them, with Aunt Raven bringing up the rear.

"Kell," he began, but she lifted her hand, holding up her index finger and effortlessly shushing him without saying a word.

"Maverick is home," Aunt Raven informed me, and my shoulders relaxed. "He's going to have a hell of a headache tomorrow, but he will be fine. Willa and Elias are watching over him until you get home."

Relief made my knees weak, thankful that he was going to be okay. He'd been so out of it after I'd had a little chat with the hookers that I'd called Aunt Raven before I called my mom. Knowing Aunt Willa and Elias were watching over him for me made me feel a little better, but I wanted to be the one taking care of him.

"Why will he have a headache?" Uncle Spider demanded, getting to his feet.

"The hooker twins shot him with a tranq," Aunt Raven told him with a shrug. "From what they showed me, it was strong enough to bring down a horse. But don't worry. He's going to be fine once it wears off."

Mom snorted derisively, causing Dad to flinch. "It's what Colt is notorious for. Drugging people to get what he wants."

I could feel the atmosphere in the room becoming more charged. I didn't know if Dad was going to get tossed out of the MC for what he'd done, and I honestly didn't give a fuck. It would be nothing less than he deserved.

But the murder in Uncle Spider's eyes as he took a step toward Dad told another story. Expulsion from the MC wouldn't be enough for him. He wanted blood.

Uncle Bash put his arm out, stopping the enforcer from taking another step. "No. River asked to deliver his punishment." He glanced around. "All in favor of River handling this?"

There was a hesitant pause before the majority of the brothers gave their affirmation, including my uncles and Maverick's dad.

TWENTY-ONE
RIVER

After I'd first found Maverick at the motel, I'd thought about what punishment I would dole out if Uncle Bash and the brothers gave me permission. But I hadn't let myself completely believe they would actually allow it.

Now that I stood in front of them all, the power to do as I wanted to my dad at my fingertips, I realized that while he deserved to be stripped of his cut for going against the brotherhood code the MC always strived to uphold, I couldn't do that to him. Because I knew that Angel's Halo was too much a part of who he was. While he'd had no qualms about hurting Maverick and me—and breaking my heart—I couldn't do the same to him.

I felt Mom, Aunt Quinn, and Aunt Raven step up behind me, the three of them offering me the support I suddenly felt desperate for as I stood there in front of Dad. For a moment, I saw a flash of real dread in his green eyes, and I knew he was wondering just how vengeful I was going to be.

"Don't worry, Dad," I told him as I willed my heart not to ache as I delivered his punishment. "I'm not going to make you turn over your cut. After all, Maverick and I kept our relationship from you for years. What you did tonight, do you think that cancels out his not telling you about us?"

"By MC standards? Yes." A muscle in his jaw started clenching and unclenching. "By my standards as your father? Not even close."

I nodded, having known that would probably be his answer. "Yeah, I get that too." I inhaled slowly, fighting the sting of tears, but failing to keep them at bay. "Then that makes this so much easier. Because what I'm going to make you give up is *me,* Dad."

He jerked as if I'd stabbed him. "What?"

"You heard me," I choked out, as a tear spilled over my lashes. "You made your choice. Your anger, it's too much for me. You can't accept Maverick and me. Now, I'm making my choice—I choose Maverick. I will always pick him. Over you or Mom or anyone else. Always."

"River, you can't—" He broke off, his face turning to stone. "If you give me up, you're giving up your mother too."

"The fuck you say!" Mom exploded. "Just because you fucked up and she's cutting you out of her life, doesn't mean I will be put in the same category. Because I'm telling you right now, Colt. If you make me choose, you're not going to like who I pick."

Sweat broke out on his brow, but that didn't stop him from calling her bluff. "You wouldn't."

"Is that a dare?" she asked in a deceptively soft voice. "I carried her inside my body. I felt her kicks and fell in love with her in a way that no man could ever possibly understand because he will never know that kind of miracle. You? You own my heart, but I will walk away from you with zero regrets if it means keeping my daughter in my life. Unlike my own mother, I will always pick my child over anyone. Including you."

He seemed to be having difficulty swallowing for a moment. "Kelli, I...I wouldn't make you choose." He scrubbed his hands over his face in agitation. "Fuck, can we just calm down for a minute here? This is getting out of control. I...I'll accept your relationship with Maverick, okay?" He gulped, his fear over losing Mom making his eyes wild. "I won't pull any more shit like I did tonight."

I gave him a sad smile as yet another tear spilled free. "If you'd accepted it before you broke my heart, that would have been great, Dad. But now, it's too little, too late." Turning my back on him, I caught Mom's hand. "I'm not asking you to choose between him and me. I would never do that to you."

Tears filled her eyes. "I know, sweetheart. But I will always pick you. Without hesitation. Please, if nothing else, I hope you understand that."

My heart only ached more. That was only one of many differences between her and Dad. "I know," I whispered.

Knowing if I stayed a moment longer, I was going to break down sobbing like a baby, I walked toward the door.

"River, stop."

The plea in Dad's voice didn't give me pause. Even when he yelled for me to wait, I kept walking, but at the door, I glanced back, only to see my aunts and Mom standing like a fortified wall in front of him, blocking him from following me.

"Goodbye, Dad."

MAVERICK WAS SNORING AWAY when I got back to the apartment. Figuring he would most likely sleep through the night, I sent Aunt Willa and Elias home. After locking up behind them, I took a long hot shower, needing to wash the events of the day off me.

But as I crawled into bed beside my man, I couldn't stop the tears from spilling over again. I cuddled up beside Mav and just let go. The anger, the heartache, the fear of losing the only person who mattered to me, it all bubbled together and boiled over until I couldn't even breathe, I was sobbing so hard.

Maverick stirred, his arms instinctively going around me and holding me. Even in his drugged-out state, his first thought was to protect and comfort me.

Not wanting to disturb him, I tried to keep quiet, but it was like attempting to contain a tsunami. Even though my brain told me he needed to rest, my body knew it was safe with him, and I couldn't control myself.

"I'm sorry," he murmured groggily, kissing the top of my head as he stroked my hair with a heavy hand. "Whatever I did, I'm sorry. I-I'll fix it, I swear."

I wiped my nose on his T-shirt. "Y-you h-have nothing t-to be s-s-sorry for," I sobbed.

"Then...what's wrong?" he asked, confusion thick in his voice.

I didn't think his drug-fogged mind would understand if I tried to explain everything to him right then. Gulping down my tears, I sat up and patted my legs. "Put your head here," I instructed, wiping my eyes with the back of my hand.

He didn't hesitate to pillow his head on my lap. When my nails stroked over his scalp as I combed them through his hair, he released a content moan. Moments later, his breathing evened out and he was asleep once again.

I sat there all night, doing nothing more than touching

him in some shape or form. He woke a few times, groaning that he had cottonmouth or that his head ached, but each time I asked if he wanted me to get him something, he grumbled something unintelligible and drifted right back to sleep.

As dawn peeked weakly through the curtains, I finally forced myself to move. My body ached from sitting in one spot for so long without moving, and my eyes felt dry and gritty, but sleep still eluded me. Carefully, I lifted Maverick's head off my lap and climbed out of bed.

In the bathroom, I found him some aspirin, then went into the kitchen to get him a bottle of water. After placing it on the nightstand, I went back to the kitchen to make coffee.

I was standing by the sink drinking my second cup when Maverick stumbled in. His eyes were bloodshot, and his skin had a pasty color to it, making me think he was feeling sick to his stomach. Crossing to me, he took the mug from my hands and drained the nearly full cup of coffee.

Blurry-eyed, he set the cup on the counter and grabbed my hips, pressing his forehead to mine. "I'm sorry."

I leaned into him. "For?"

"Whatever I did yesterday. I can't remember shit, baby. But if I hurt you, or said anything, or did anything…" He groaned. "I'm so sorry."

My hands touched his bare back under his shirt as I wrapped my arms around his middle. "You didn't do anything wrong. I'm the one who should be saying sorry. My dad…" I swallowed the fresh lump of emotion trying to choke me and blinked back the sting of tears. My eyes ached from all the tears I'd shed the day before, and I'd thought I was all dried up, but apparently not. "But we don't have to worry about him anymore."

He pulled back so he could look down at me. "Please

tell me you didn't kill him. I can barely see right now, babe. I don't think I could bury a body this morning."

Despite feeling like I was going to burst into tears at any moment, I lifted my lips in a small grin. "No," I rasped out. "I didn't kill him or anyone else. He was breathing the last time I saw him."

"Then what happened?" he asked with a frown.

I shrugged. "I cut him out of my life. From this day on, he doesn't exist to me."

"River…" One of his hands cupped the side of my face. "Baby, I know that you're pissed right now. Fuck, so am I. But you are going to regret this. I can't let you—"

"Stop," I whispered. "What he did? He basically made me choose, and I picked you. I will never regret that. The way he was acting, how he was treating you, it was becoming toxic. And I'm already tired of it all. If we're going to get married and start our own family, I refuse to let that shit touch our kids."

"But—"

"I still have the rest of my family. My mom, aunts, uncles, cousins. They are still very much a part of my life. But not him. He lost me the moment he paid those bitches to drug you." My tears spilled free, and I hurriedly wiped them away when I saw his eyes darken at the sight of them.

"But he's your dad," he murmured. "I know you love him."

"I love you more," I interrupted. Forcing a smile, I lifted onto my tiptoes and gave him a quick kiss. "I need to get ready. I have a doctor's appointment in an hour."

While I got ready, I finally turned my phone back on. I'd turned it off the night before when Dad had started blowing it up on my way home. He had nothing to say I wanted to hear, and I still wasn't interested in anything that came out of his mouth. But I figured my mom or Maverick's would want an update on how he was feeling.

As soon as my screen lit up, it started going crazy with all the missed text and calls. The majority were, of course, from Dad, but I deleted them before I could second=guess myself. Cutting him out of my life wasn't just a ruse to get him to do what I wanted. I'd meant it, and I wasn't going to give in just because he was suddenly sorry for what he'd done.

I didn't trust him any longer. My faith in his love for me had turned to ashes the day before, and I wasn't ever going to give him a second chance to break my heart again. Maybe it was harsh, and maybe I might even feel a twinge of regret later on down the road, but I refused to let anything toxic touch my life any longer.

From now on, I was going to focus on healing. My heart was already battered and bruised from miscarrying my baby. But now, part of it was also shattered and missing, thanks to my father.

Before I got dressed, I texted both Mom and Aunt Willa to let them know Maverick was awake and out of bed. I shot Mila a quick message to remind her that I had a doctor's appointment and that I might not get to the store until closer to dinnertime. I had graduation practice that afternoon that I really didn't feel like going to, but I had been warned if I didn't show up for it, I couldn't walk with the rest of my class the next day.

Pulling on jeans and a T-shirt, I scooped my hair up into a ponytail and walked out of our bedroom to find Maverick sitting on the couch with his phone to his ear. He was leaning forward, his elbow propped on his knee while he pressed the palm of his hand into one eye socket like his head was throbbing.

"I said I'm fine," he was muttering into the receiver. "River has a thing this morning, and then once she goes to practice, I'll be there. Yeah..." He paused, listening to whoever was on the other end. "I know, man. Fuck. Okay. I'll see you then."

Lowering his hand, he glared down at his phone for a moment before lifting his head. Seeing me standing there, he quickly dropped his gaze back to the screen. "Give me ten to shower and change, and I'll be ready to go, baby."

I sighed. "You don't have to keep things from me."

"I'm not," he denied. But we knew each other too well. I knew all his tells, so I could read him as easily as if he were an open book. The guilt that flashed momentarily in his gray eyes told me all I needed to know.

"Please don't lie to me either." I crossed to the couch and climbed onto his lap. Cupping his face in both of my hands, I leaned in and kissed him. "Listen to me. You don't have to cut anyone out of your life. I'm not asking that of you. I know Dad is still your MC brother. I respect that. But I'm asking you right now, don't start hiding shit. Don't lie to me. And please, babe, please respect my decision to cut him out of my life."

His groan was loaded with frustration. "I just want you to be happy."

"Mav, my heart is one big ache right now," I told him honestly, causing his jaw to clench. "Between the baby and now Dad? I'm going to need a little time to heal. Okay?" After a slight hesitation, he nodded, and I began to relax a little. "Thank you."

Standing, I walked toward the kitchen. "I'll grab us to-go cups of coffee while you get ready."

TWENTY-TWO

MAVERICK

Stopping my bike in front of the clubhouse, I refused to feel guilty over what I was about to do.

River said she wanted nothing to do with her dad, but I knew my girl too well. At the moment, she was pissed and hurting. But in a week, or a month—fuck, maybe even in a year—she would wake up one morning and miss Colt so much, it would hurt her all over again. And as her man, I couldn't just sit back and let that happen.

When her dad had called me that morning, asking for a face-to-face, I knew I had to straighten all of this out between the two of them.

Pocketing my keys, I adjusted my cut and walked into the clubhouse. The place was never empty. There was always a brother in residence and a few sheep to take care of their needs. When I walked in, Jack and Kingston were sitting on one of the couches, watching some sports talk show.

Seeing me, Kingston stood, his face dark with concern. "How is she?"

"Pissed. Hurting. Trying to tell me that she's fine." My jaw clenched. "She's at graduation practice right now."

Jack was slower to stand, turning off the television set as he nodded toward the stairs that led up to Uncle Bash's office. "He's up there. All the dads are. And they are pissed."

I exhaled slowly. "Whatever happens, tell my girl I love her."

Kingston slapped me on the back as the three of us started for the steps. "Bro, they aren't pissed at you. I seriously thought your pops was going to take Uncle Colt's head off last night at Church. He's lucky my mom, Aunt Raven, and Aunt Kelli showed up, or he'd probably be dead right now."

Cursing under my breath, I knocked on the closed office door and heard a barked, "Come in," before opening it. Squaring my shoulders, I stepped into the room, my eyes automatically clocking everyone and where they were.

Uncle Bash was behind his desk, my dad standing behind him on his left, Uncle Hawk on his right. Uncle Jet and Uncle Raider were in seats in front of the desk, while Matt and Tanner Reid stood against the wall, their gazes following the man who was pacing in front of them.

After a few more steps, Colt finally turned to face me. His face was set in hard lines, but pale. His green eyes, so like his daughter's, were just as bloodshot as hers had been that morning, with dark shadows beneath them that gave him a depraved, haunted vibe.

Kingston and Jack flanked me, and I was thankful for their support as they stood behind me. Colt's gaze locked with mine, and I crossed my arms over my chest, staring him down as he seemed to struggle to find words.

He was the one who'd asked for this meeting. I'd come

out of respect to him as a brother, but more than anything because I wanted to fix the rift between him and my girl.

"It's two fucking words," Dad barked. "Repeat after me —I'm sorry. Not hard to say, dickhead."

Colt's jaw worked for a moment before he finally unclenched it enough to mutter, "I'm sorry."

"You know, your plan was pretty genius," I complimented him. "You just didn't take into consideration one important aspect. River has been the only female I've seen from the moment I hit puberty. She knows more than anyone that I would rather chop off my own cock than touch anyone else."

He grunted. "Yeah, well, I thought this whole bullshit relationship between you two was just you trying to fuck with me. I didn't like you using my little girl to prank me. I didn't realize you two had been together for years."

I stood up straighter. "Our relationship isn't bullshit. I've loved her since before I even understood what that kind of love really meant." I pulled my brows together as I considered what else he'd just said. "And why the hell would I prank you like that? If I wanted to fuck with you, I wouldn't use River. Trust me, old man. I have better ways to jerk you around than using the woman I love as bait."

"Yeah," Kingston muttered behind me. "If I were you, Unc, I wouldn't be going to Mav for ink anytime soon. He's liable to give you a big hairy cock or something."

Colt's lips twitched in amusement. "Noted."

"When I asked you for permission to date River on her birthday, what I really wanted to ask was for your blessing to marry her," I told him, needing to lay it all on the table so he understood where I was coming from. Maybe I should have just asked him that day instead of easing into it like Jack and Kingston had suggested. "Even though she's vowed to cut you out of her life, I would still like your blessing."

His jaw tensed again, and I witnessed him having trouble swallowing for a moment before he blew out a harsh sigh. "Yeah, boy. You have my blessing." He thrust his hands into his jeans pockets. "But I want to walk her down the aisle."

"I can't guarantee that, man." I gave it to him straight. "She's stubborn, and right now, she's pissed. You broke her heart."

His shoulders slumped, his throat working again as he fought his emotions. "I know."

"Well, don't just stand there, dumbass!" Uncle Jet grumbled. "Figure out how to fix it. You found a way to get Kelli to forgive you for all the shit you put her through. I'm sure you can sort this out."

Colt sighed. "Kelli suggested a few ways that might win River over, but I don't know if she'll accept anything I do. Or if it would even be enough. That girl is worse than her mother. She can hold a grudge."

"You never know unless you at least try." Uncle Bash spoke for the first time. "You shitheads take a seat. We'll do what we can to help."

"SHE'S GOING to think you're trying to buy her forgiveness," I growled at my future father-in-law as he suggested what he wanted to do to win River back.

"You take her on vacation, and by the time you return, the repairs on that house will be done," Colt argued.

"She wants us to fix it up ourselves," I told him. "It was why we even put in an offer on that house. She loves that place and has all these do-it-yourself projects planned. You need to think of something that doesn't involve money."

His eyes went blank, and I could tell he was clueless as to what that even meant.

"Okay, Unc," Kingston spoke up, trying to help. "Let me try to simplify this for you. What's River's favorite movie?"

He frowned, his brain working on overdrive as he tried to find the answer. "I got nothin'."

"Her favorite color?"

"Blue." He was quick to answer this time.

"You only know that because I told you at her party," Dad said with another glare. "And her favorite movie is *The Princess Bride.*"

"How the fuck do you know all that about my kid?" he demanded angrily.

"She spent more time at my house as a kid than at yours," the enforcer said with a shrug.

"And when she wasn't at Spider's, she was at mine," Uncle Raider added. "I lost count of the times River made Kingston watch that princess movie with her. Got Quinn hooked on it, too. I get them both themed presents from the movie every year for Christmas. Don't you pay attention?"

"I..." His eyes grew damp, but he quickly looked away, hiding his emotions from us all. "I guess I don't."

"Okay, asshole, once we fix this thing between you and River, I think you need to start taking that girl on a father-daughter date once a week," Uncle Jet suggested. "I take Nova out every Sunday if possible. We go to a movie, have dinner, and then get dessert. And she tells me all about her week. Even when I don't have two minutes to spare, I still make it work."

"Yeah," I agreed with a nod, liking that idea. "I bet she would like that."

His green gaze snapped to me, the tears gone and replaced by a glimmer of hope. "You think so?"

"It will be a step in the right direction," I affirmed. "But first, we have to get her to forgive you. And like I said, you buying us that house or paying to have it remodeled isn't going to work. Dropping some cash isn't going to repair the damage already done to her heart. She needs a big gesture that comes from your love for her, not your wallet."

Frustration tightened his face, and he got to his feet so he could start pacing again. "I don't know what to do to show her without buying her something. It's what I've always done."

"Then don't expect an invitation to the wedding," I told him point-blank. "There's a difference between saying sorry and actually making amends. And that is exactly what you have to do this time."

"You have to show her a big gesture," Jack suggested. "Something that shows her that you're going to take her relationship with Maverick seriously. That you respect them as a couple." He pushed away from the wall where he'd been standing and observing us for the past half hour. Jack had always been the quiet one of the Hannigan offspring. The one who sat back and observed, and who didn't talk unless he had something important to say. So, when he did speak, everyone usually shut up and listened. "I have an idea, but it's going to take some fast moving, and we'll need Aunt Raven and the other women to help."

TWENTY-THREE

RIVER

Holding my diploma in one hand and my cap in the other, I pushed through the crowd of my fellow students and their families in search of my own.

All throughout the ceremony, Garett had sat beside me grumbling about how boring the whole thing was. I couldn't have agreed more, and all I wanted was for the damn thing to be over so I could find Maverick and go home.

While I was at practice the day before, Mav had been sent on a run for the MC, and so the plans I'd had for us to spend the night getting as little sleep as possible had been ruined. He promised he'd be back in time for my graduation, but I hadn't seen him before the ceremony started. When my name was called, however, I heard him cheering for me the loudest, and I had glanced out at the auditorium to find him sitting with my parents and the rest of my extended family.

But as I walked through the crowds, I couldn't find anyone, not even an aunt or uncle. Frustrated, I fished my phone out of the pocket of the dress I was wearing under my gown and called Maverick.

It rang three times before he answered. "Hey, babe. There was a problem at the clubhouse. I didn't want it to ruin your and Garett's graduation party, so I'm going to take care of it myself."

"Oh," I said with a pout. "Will it take long? I missed you."

"Mila and Monroe are waiting for you in the parking lot. They're going to doll you up at the store and then bring you over." His voice dropped. "I missed you too."

"But I don't want to be dolled up," I complained. "I don't even want to go to a party. Can't we just have our own celebration at home?"

I heard his agonized groan. "Soon, baby. I swear, very, very soon."

"Fine," I grumbled, stomping toward the parking lot. "But we aren't staying long at that stupid party."

"See you soon. Love you."

"I love you too." Hanging up, I looked around for any sign of the twins. Spotting one of Monroe's bodyguards, I marched toward them.

The guard stood outside of a monster of an SUV. The thing was bulletproof, probably even bazooka-proof if Gian had his way. The thought made my lips twitch as I approached. The guard turned and opened the back door, and I saw the twins inside already laughing and seeming to be having a good time.

Before I climbed in beside them, I took off the gown and folded it over my arm, then slid in beside Mila.

"That dress is pretty," Monroe commented, handing me a glass of champagne.

"Thanks." I tossed back the contents of the glass before holding it out for a refill. If I had to wait to get my man alone, I planned on having a nice buzz going on beforehand.

Mila poured me half a glass, and I only glared at her until she topped it off. "That's your last glass until after you get ready," she informed me.

"Whatever," I grumbled unhappily as the driver pulled into the slow flow of traffic leaving the school.

"I know you wanted to go home and bone my brother," my best friend said with a wicked grin. "But he's got plans of his own. He wants to make today special. It's important to him."

Guilt hit me dead center, and I lost my pout. "Okay, okay. I'll try my best. But I'm just..."

"Horny?" she supplied, making Monroe snort the expensive champagne out her nose and causing us to burst out laughing.

"Yeah," I said while Monroe coughed and tried to get the bubbles out of her sinus cavity. "I haven't been without it this long since I was fifteen."

One of the guards turned in the front seat, making sure Monroe was okay, but we shooed him away, already taking care of her. The drive to the store was quick and full of more laughter from the three of us.

The store was already decked out and ready for our grand opening, but we still had a few things left to do before we could let customers in. When we walked in, Aunt Willa and Mom were already waiting with two younger women I recognized from the twins' double wedding. They'd done their hair and makeup for the event and were supposedly makeup artists to the stars.

"This is a little much, don't you think?" I muttered as Mom grabbed my hand and tugged me over to the corner where we'd set up the nursing mother's area. "It's just a party."

"Maverick wants everything perfect," Aunt Willa said

as she sat down across from me. Mom took the seat beside her, and the two women clasped hands while keeping their eyes glued to me. It was a weird picture for me to witness. Aunt Willa was all kinds of huggy, but Mom, not so much. Yet the two of them were practically clinging to each other's hands.

"Is everything okay?" I asked, concerned.

"It's great," Mom said with a small smile. "You just sit there and be pampered."

I sighed and glanced around for Mila. "I need more champagne!"

"Coming up," she called from somewhere in the store. "Just getting your dress options for the party sorted out."

"You're all acting really weird." I lifted my brows at the two moms. "Have you guys been drinking?"

"Maybe," Mom said with a wink. "Like I said, just sit there and be pampered. Don't you worry about us, little girl."

When my hair was done, the other woman started on my makeup, but I wasn't allowed to look in a mirror to see how I looked. Muttering under my breath at how crazy everyone was acting, I stood with my champagne glass in hand and went to get dressed.

The moms followed Mila and me into one of the huge dressing rooms in the back. We'd wanted to make them spacious enough that a mother could take her stroller and toddler into them and still have room to move around freely. With the five of us in the room, we still had plenty of space to stretch out.

But as I walked in and saw the selection of dresses hanging on the wall, I realized that we weren't just going to a party.

"Where did you get wedding dresses?" I demanded, turning to frown at the four women.

"Lyric knows someone," Mila said with a casual shrug. "I ordered ones I thought you might like in your size. We can send back the ones you don't choose. The only problem is these all came off the rack because it was so last minute. So, the fit might not be the greatest."

Suddenly, the realization of what was actually happening hit me, and my eyes filled with tears. "Mav planned a surprise wedding?"

"No tears," Mom commanded, pointing her finger in my face, but I saw how glassy her own eyes were. "You'll make me cry too, not to mention, you'll ruin your makeup."

The twins hugged me from either side. "You need to pick a dress," Mila reminded me. "I know it's a hard decision to make, but we are kind of running out of time. I promised my brother we would get you to the clubhouse by a certain hour, or he will come looking for you."

Sucking in a deep breath, I blinked back my tears and glanced at the dresses again. "I always thought we would run off to Vegas and get married in one of those little chapels, so I never really thought about a wedding dress before." But I couldn't say I was unhappy to have to pick one out now.

"There's nothing wrong with that," Aunt Willa said. "That's what James and I did."

"It was just your dad and me on a beach in Hawaii," Mom reminisced. "I had a simple silk dress and was barefoot. It was perfect."

The mention of my dad made my heart hurt, but I pushed down all thoughts of him and focused on the dress options.

One was a huge ballgown-like dress, while another was

mermaid-style. But my gaze kept returning to the one with double spaghetti straps. The top was a mixture of floral lace and pearls that extended down to about the waist. The bottom was a slinky, crepe skirt that flowed into scalloped edging, with more of the floral lace for the train. It was the perfect blend of old-school Hollywood elegance mixed with a touch of contemporary that had me falling in love with it before I'd even tried it on.

Mom noticed my gaze returning to it again and again, and she walked over to take it off the wall. "Don't just stand there, little girl. You won't know if it looks good on you or not, just looking at it on the hanger."

With a happy squeak, I pulled off the dress I'd worn to graduation and then let the others help me into the white dress. When I turned to look at myself in the mirror, fresh tears stung my eyes. "Is there a veil, by any chance?" I asked Mila.

"They sent a veil for each of the options," she assured me. "Hold tight. I'll get it."

AN HOUR LATER, after Mila and Monroe both changed into bridesmaid dresses, we got into the limo that was waiting for us and rode over to the clubhouse. The parking lot was packed with cars and motorcycles.

Excitement was already making me jittery, but realizing that I was walking into the clubhouse as River Hannigan and walking out as River Masterson made me dizzy with happiness. The others got out of the limo first, and then Mom turned to help me so I didn't wrinkle my dress.

The twins and Aunt Willa rushed in to make sure everything was in order, while Mom stayed outside with me. The sun was starting to set, and I was glad it wasn't raining like it had been on the twins' wedding day. As the door closed behind the others, Mom turned and took my hands.

"Maverick helped plan today, but he's not the one who made it possible," my mother informed me, her face suddenly very serious. "Your dad did."

I stiffened and took a step back from her reflexively. "No, he wouldn't. He's been nothing but an asshole since he found out about my relationship with Maverick. And then the other night…" I was getting pissed just thinking about what had happened to Maverick.

"I know, sweetheart. Believe me, more than anyone, I know." She gave me an imploring look. "But your dad is sorry. He's trying to make amends and show you that he accepts your relationship now."

I didn't believe her. My dad was too stubborn to do a complete 180 like that and suddenly be on board with me being with Maverick. Not wanting to argue with her about it, I turned and walked back to the limo, tempted to get in and let the driver take me as far away from all of this as fast as he could. But as my hand touched the door handle, I stopped.

No, damn it. I was not going to walk away. Not when the man I loved was waiting for me in the clubhouse. Marrying him was my dream, and it honestly didn't matter to me how it happened, as long as I *did* happen. Why should I let my feelings for my father ruin it?

Determinedly, I turned to go back, only to find Mom was now gone.

Dad stood where she'd been only moments before, dressed in dress slacks, a white button-up, and his leather MC cut. There was a vulnerable, almost pleading look in his eyes that hurt me to see, but I crossed my arms over my chest and glared at him.

For the longest time, we stayed just like that, both of us too stubborn to look away or be the first to break the silence. The sun was almost completely set before he cleared his throat. "You look beautiful, sweetheart," he choked out.

"Did you come to stop the wedding?" I demanded instead of accepting his compliment.

His throat bobbed before he shook his head. "No, River. I heard Kelli tell you that I was the one to set all of this up. Why would I stop something I want to happen?"

I shrugged. "Because you wanted me to get my hopes up. Then, at the last minute, pull the plug on it all."

"No, I'm not going to do that. I realize how much Maverick means to you now. If I'd realized before—" He broke off, a muscle in his jaw working for a moment before he could speak again. "I'm so sorry for what I did. I know it doesn't make any sense to you, but when the boy asked to date you, I thought he was just bullshitting me. I didn't like him playing with you to get a reaction out of me. I honestly didn't know how serious you two were about each other."

"He's my life. I would do anything for him."

"And I see now that he would do anything for you, too." He gave me a grim smile. "I've realized I don't know anything about you, River. And I'm sorry about that more than anything. I guess I stopped paying attention some-where over the years, and for the life of me, I can't remember when or even why. Maybe if I'd opened my eyes sooner, I would have noticed how you felt about the boy."

Tears blinded me, and I quickly blinked them away, not wanting him to see them. "It only took you losing me to open them."

"I know, and I'm sorry. But you, more than anyone, should know how stubborn I am." He tried to grin, but even through my tears, I could see it was more of a pained twist of his lips. "You're just as bad. Where did you think you got it from?"

"Mom."

"Okay, so you got equal parts of our stubbornness," he conceded with a snort. But the noise turned into an agonized sound when a tear broke free and dripped down my cheek. "I-I would like the chance to get to know you now, if it's not too late. Maybe..." He stopped and swallowed hard a few times before he was able to continue. "Maybe we could have dinner once a week, just the two of us."

"I..." I stopped and pressed my lips together, holding on to my angry words at the sight of his own tears spilling over his lashes. Seeing his pain gave me no joy. If anything, it only made my broken heart ache more. "I don't know," I muttered instead. "Maybe."

"I realize winning back your trust and forgiveness will take time, River. I'm just asking for a chance."

"I-I'll think about it," I offered.

"While you're thinking, could I walk you down the aisle?" he asked. His voice was so full of hope, and with his tears still falling freely, I found myself nodding.

Dad lifted his hand toward the front door of the clubhouse. "After you, sweetheart."

Holding the train of my dress, I walked into the clubhouse. Mom and the twins were right inside, and the three of them rushed to get me cleaned up since my tears had messed up my makeup.

The music started, and my heart jumped into my throat. It took every ounce of willpower I had not to run into the common room and rush into Maverick's arms. A simple "I do" from the both of us and we would be married. But if he'd helped set all this up, with Mayor Jenkins even getting our marriage license taken care of so it wouldn't ruin the surprise, that must have meant he wanted a wedding shared with our family and friends, so I wasn't going to ruin it for him.

Kingston was waiting to walk my mom down the aisle, and then the twins followed behind them. When it was our turn, Dad offered me his arm, and I hesitated for a moment before finally placing my hand through it.

I was still mad, and my heart still ached, but I knew he was trying. His walking me down the aisle meant a lot to me. It showed me that he had accepted that Maverick was my forever.

Unlike at Mila and Monroe's wedding, the clubhouse wasn't overflowing with people. Lyric's huge extended family had all come, and the building had been bursting at the seams with a mixture of rockers and bikers. Now, there were only bikers, which meant there was room for chairs, so the guests could sit.

As Dad and I started down the aisle, everyone stood and faced us. I heard several people close to us murmuring how beautiful I looked, but I was too entranced by the sight at the end of the aisle to pay attention.

Maverick stood there, Kingston and Jack at his side, wearing a suit for the first time in his life—but, of course, his cut was on over it. His hair was pushed back from his face, and he'd shaved. I'd never seen him look more handsome than he did right then. His gray eyes ate up the sight of me in my wedding dress, and I watched as he struggled to swallow.

Halfway down the aisle, he lost the battle against his tears and the first one spilled free, but he didn't lower his gaze or try to hide them from me. His smile was trembly but so full of love that my own tears started to flow again.

It felt like it took forever to reach him, but it was only a matter of seconds. And then the minister was asking who was giving me away.

I held my breath as the entire clubhouse seemed to fill with tension. I'd been worried about this part from the moment I'd agreed to let Dad walk me down the aisle, wondering if he would actually let Maverick have me. The two men I cared about the most in the world stared each other down, and then Dad offered Mav his hand. The two shook, then my dad pulled Maverick in for a hard, backslapping hug.

I was blinded by my tears, and by some miracle, I was able to hold back my happy sob as the hug ended and Dad placed my hand in Maverick's. At the feel of his touch, everything and everyone in the room seemed to disappear. Not even the minister existed for me except when he instructed me to repeat my vows.

It was just Maverick and me, the way it had always been. The way it always would be.

I slid the ring on to Mav's finger then had to hold back a sob when he did the same. It was official. Nothing could ever come between us. Nothing and no one could take him from me now.

He'd always been mine, and now the world knew it.

TWENTY-FOUR
MAVERICK

As soon as the driver closed the door of the limo, I had River's dress up over her hips. She was already soaked, her pussy lips glistening with her need for me, and it took me a second to truly grasp how perfect this moment was.

I felt like I'd been waiting my entire life for this day, to show the world that she was mine—that she fucking chose me.

She could have had any motherfucker she wanted, but I was the lucky bastard who got to be her man.

Her fingers were already working on my pants. The moment her hand wrapped around my shaft, I threw my head back, groaning at how good her touch was. It had been too goddamn long since I'd last had her, but I hadn't wanted to chance hurting her. Staying away the night before after the doctor had given us the green light at her appointment had been one of the hardest things I'd ever had to do. "Baby, put me in you," I pleaded. "I can't wait."

She bit her lip, hesitation suddenly on her beautiful face

when she'd been just as desperate for me as I was for her only seconds before. "What if...?"

My heart stopped, and I cupped her face. "I'll respect whatever you decide. There's protection in my wallet. But if you want to try..."

Sucking her bottom lip between her teeth, she considered the options for a moment before lifting up and then guiding my cock into her tight little body. "If it's meant to be, it will happen," she said on a moan as my girth stretched her pussy walls. "I won't be scared if you promise to hold me the whole time."

I clenched my hands on her hips as her body welcomed me back by squeezing my shaft like a tight, silky fist. "Baby, I'll hold you for the rest of my life," I vowed through gritted teeth. "I love you so fucking much. I will protect you and our family until my last breath."

Her hands went to my shoulders to steady herself, and I helped her ride me as the limo drove us toward Hannigans'. Her walls started to contract around me, trying to trigger my own release as she threw her head back and screamed my name. "That's it, wife," I growled, lifting and dropping her on my throbbing cock faster. "Come all over your husband's cock, baby."

Her pussy pulsed even harder, making me see spots at how good it felt, and I came harder than I ever had in my life.

Breathing hard, she lifted her head just as the limo began to slow, a grin on her face. "That was a great first ride as a married couple, but I'm going to want more." Her eyes darkened hungrily. "Soon."

"As a wedding present, Gian and Monroe are lending us their jet to fly to Mexico tonight for our honeymoon," I informed her. "Tonight, I'm going to make love to my beautiful wife, listening to the ocean waves crash against the beach."

"That sounds perfect," she breathed, rubbing herself against me for a moment, teasing me before lifting off my cock and fixing her dress.

"No panties?" I asked with a frown, realizing there hadn't been any to take off her earlier.

"They would have caused a line," she said with a smirk.

"Fuck," I muttered, rubbing a hand over my face. "Now that's all I'm going to be thinking about. You can't dance with any guy who isn't related to you by blood or marriage."

Her sexy laugh made my cock twitch as I stuffed myself back into my pants. Once we were both presentable again, I opened the door and stepped out before helping her.

Most of the guests were already inside the bar when we walked in. The four-tiered cake Kingston had helped his mom make sat on a table by itself in a corner. As soon as everyone noticed we'd arrived, we were swarmed by people congratulating us. I pulled River closer, growling at any of my MC brothers who tried to hug her who weren't related to her in some way.

For the next hour, we were constantly surrounded by people wishing us well, and all I really wanted was to get my wife alone again. Every few minutes, I would check the time, wondering if it was too soon to leave for the airport.

"You can't leave until you cut the cake," Mila hissed to me when she noticed what I was doing for the fifth time in as many minutes. "Mom will murder you if you even try."

"It would be worth it," I whispered back just as Colt came up to us.

Nervously, he held out his hand to his daughter. "I was hoping for a dance."

River stared at his hand for a long moment before giving

a ghost of her usually bright smile and placing her much smaller hand in his. "I'd like that."

I released the breath I hadn't realized I was holding as they stepped onto the makeshift dance floor. I honestly hadn't known if River would let her dad walk her down the aisle earlier or not. It had been her choice, which was why I'd stayed inside and hadn't tried to convince her one way or the other. It had to be her choice, just like having a relationship with him going forward would be.

As I watched them dance, I saw Mom looking at them wistfully, and I walked over to ask her for a dance. Her gray eyes lit up, and she practically dragged me out onto the dance floor. Laughing, I tucked her close and began to sway to the music as other father-daughter and mother-son couples joined us.

Lexa and Uncle Bash passed us as they took to the dance floor, while Uncle Jet and Nova followed. Kingston swept his mom into a dip, making her sweet giggles fill the bar. Jack looked stiff as he danced with Aunt Gracie, but she looked so happy that I couldn't laugh at my brother for how uncomfortable he seemed.

"Raven is pouting," Mom murmured, glancing around with a frown. "I wonder where Max is..." Her voice drifted off as her gaze landed on the door as it opened.

Max was just entering, but unlike at the wedding, he wasn't alone now. At his side was a girl I'd never seen before. She was gorgeous, with a mass of dark hair and golden skin that had to be natural. Her dark eyes glanced around the room in a mixture of fear and wonder as she kept one hand in Max's and the other fidgeted with the skirt of her dress.

The girl stopped walking after they'd come several yards into the bar, and Max looked down at her with concern. Releasing her hand, he moved his own as he spoke to her using sign language. He'd taken American Sign Language as his language elective in high school, and his mom had taught him the basics when we were all kids. I didn't know a lot of it, but I did know the bare necessities, and it looked like he was telling her not to be scared.

A gasp to my left had my head shooting around to find Aunt Kelli staring at them as if she'd seen a ghost. Not observing any possible danger to her or anyone else, I shifted my gaze to my wife, but her eyes were on the newcomers as well. Noting her frown, I stopped dancing, needing to fix whatever was putting that look on her face.

"Mom." Max's deep voice reached us, and everyone in the bar was suddenly looking at where he and the girl at his side were now facing Aunt Raven. He signed the words as he spoke, "This is Delaney." His electric-blue gaze zoomed around the room, glaring at all the guys before settling back on Delaney and softening. "And she's mine."

EPILOGUE

River

I smiled at the customer as I handed over her bag. The woman had come in an hour before to "browse." She'd started by looking through our baby section, telling Avery that her niece was having a little girl in a few months and she wanted to check out our selections so she could report back to the girl.

But then, she'd just had to look at our more intimate selection because her son was getting married, and she wanted to maybe bring her future daughter-in-law in to shop for their honeymoon.

It wasn't much longer before she was in our eighteen-and-over-only section, where she'd then selected a few personal items—and a few things for her husband's pleasure as well. The poor woman had been beet red as she'd placed her purchases on the counter for me to ring up.

And only after the other customers had left.

I thought it was adorable, but unnecessary. There was no shame in coming in just for those items, but it seemed like a good percentage of our clientele was embarrassed to shop for such things. At least, the first time or two. By the third or fourth time they returned to Womanland, they had no qualms about going straight to the restricted area—or even asking one of us what products we would recommend.

In the three years since Womanland had opened, we'd gotten great support for the store not just from the locals in Creswell Springs, but from our online customers as well. Lyric's female family members always came in to shop whenever they were in town to visit. When his cousin Arella and her husband Jordan had come in just a few months before, the actress had tweeted that she'd found the cutest outfit for her toddler daughter, and we'd gotten swarmed with people looking for the same outfit for their little ones. We'd sold out of everything in the store within two weeks, and our suppliers hadn't been able to keep up with the demand for a while.

"I've also included a twenty-five-percent-off coupon for your next purchase with us," I told her as she took the bag. "It's good in any and all of our departments."

If it was possible, she turned an even brighter shade of crimson as she mumbled a "thank you" and practically sprinted out of the store.

As soon as the door closed behind her, Avery burst into giggles, and I couldn't hide my own laughter as Mila came in through the back door. She'd gone over to have lunch with Lyric an hour before, but I knew she was really going to the preschool down the block where her boys spent half the day. That was a recent development, and she was still not completely okay with them being with something other than Lyric or her mom when she couldn't bring them to work with her.

"Okay, one—what's so funny?" Her gray eyes fell on me, and she put her hands on her hips. "And two—and I stress the most important question—why are you on your feet? I told my brother you would be in the office doing the book-work, and now I find that you've made a liar of me."

I rolled my eyes at her. "Oh, please. I've been up here a total of ten minutes, and most of that was for entertainment purposes. I was watching that poor woman on the security monitor flit from one section to another, and then she went into the restricted area and I knew it was going to be amusing." An angry kick hit me right behind my belly button, and I rubbed my hand over where my son was making himself known, trying to soothe his attitude. That boy was going to be just as much of a hell-raiser as either of his grandfathers.

"See!" Mila scolded, pointing her finger at me. "You're in pain."

"Of course I'm in pain!" I yelled back, frustrated with her. No one gave me any peace these days. I was three weeks out from my due date, and everyone was constantly growling at me to stay off my feet and take it easy. I needed to be productive, damn it. Sitting around doing nothing was more exhausting than anything for me. "This kid is as big as his fucking father. I have to have a C-section because he's so damn big."

My best friend's face turned contrite. "I just want you to be careful. Your doctor is on vacation and won't be back until two days before your scheduled C-section."

I nearly stamped my foot, but I stopped myself just in time, remembering the last time I'd done just that. It had only been the week before, and when I'd stomped it down, I'd peed a little. Thankfully, I kept a change of clothes in the office, because this little dude liked to play soccer with my bladder—and not in the cute way some mommies-to-be had to constantly go to the bathroom. It was more of a tidal wave effect, and not even using panty liners helped some days.

Breathing deeply through my nose, I tried to count to ten to calm my irritation. I'd been irrationally grumpy at times during the entire third trimester, but I tried my best not to take it out on those I loved the most. Mila was lucky she was one of those people, or I would have already picked up whatever was closest to me and hurled it at her head.

Unfortunately for my husband, whom I loved the most in the entire world, that didn't save him from me throwing things at his ginormous head. "I'm fine," I said through gritted teeth. "But if it makes you feel better, I will return to the prison that you call our office and finish up the stupid..." I'd taken one step in the direction of the office and felt a puddle suddenly pour out of me. "Shit. He did it again. I can't go anywhere without pissing all over the place."

"Um, I don't think that's pee," Avery mumbled in a horrified voice as she stared down at the floor.

Mila ran over, her eyes looked frightened as she bent to examine the puddle I'd just embarrassingly made. Tears filled her gray eyes as she looked up at me. "I think your water broke."

"Why are you crying?" I demanded. "All you do is cry anymore. I'm sorry I yelled, okay? God."

"I'm crying because I'm scared for you!" she shouted. "And because I'm pregnant, you jerk."

"Oh," I whispered, tears filling my own eyes. "Are you okay? How far along are you? Does Lyric know yet?"

"I'm good," she said as she straightened. "And yes, Lyric knows. He knew before I did. I'm only like six weeks, and yes, it's fucking twins. Again. I swear, this is the last time, so one of them better be a girl, because it's all the kids that man is getting to pop out of my vagina. He's getting snipped! I already made the appointment. He just doesn't know it yet."

"Um, should I call someone?" Avery asked hesitantly as she stood, anxious, beside me. "I mean, you're still leaking. It's not stopping."

"It's fine." I waved her off. "I haven't even started having contractions yet. I can finish the books. Just let me change and put on one of those adult diapers Kingston gave me as a gag a few weeks ago." He was trying to be funny at the time, but I'd actually appreciated the thought. Now I could finish the books before I had to go to the hospital.

As I turned to go back to the office to get my fresh clothes and the diaper, I called over my shoulder, "And do *not* call my husband yet. He's doing a back piece that has a lot of detail to it. I don't want him worrying about me when he needs to concentrate on that."

In the bathroom, I cleaned up and then returned to the office to finish up the bookwork. Every now and then, I would feel pressure, but it was fine. The contractions hadn't really started, so I wasn't worried.

When I was done, I shut everything down and walked out to the front of the store. Only to stop in my tracks as the first pain hit me so hard, it nearly brought me to my knees. "Fuck!" I screamed, bending in half and causing the customer in the store to stop and stare at me.

"It's only been half an hour," Mila was saying into the phone when I could breathe again. "Right, okay. We're leaving for the hospital now."

Hanging up, she pocketed the phone. "Lyric is calling everyone. Maverick will just have to reschedule the back piece." Putting her arm around me, she guided me toward the exit. "Avery, lock up. I'll let you know when baby Rocco makes an appearance."

"Good luck, River," she called.

I could barely breathe, let alone answer her. That pain had been no joke. Not even when I'd had the miscarriage had the pain been so intense, and I'd thought that had been the worst pain of my life. I'd been wrong. So, so wrong. This was worse on an entirely different scale of agony.

"My doctor," I cried when we were on the road to the hospital. "She's on vacation. Who's going to deliver the baby?" My panic was starting to set in, and I began to gasp for breath. "Oh my God! Why didn't I go to the hospital when my water first broke? I need a fucking C-section. Mila, drive faster."

She reached out and caught one of my hands in hers. "River, babe, calm down. The stress is bad for you *and* Rocco. Everything is going to be fine. I promise. Just take a few deep breaths with me. In...and out. Deep air in...slow breath out."

I followed her instructions and felt some of the panic ease. Rubbing my hands over my stomach, I began talking to my son. "I'm so sorry. I wanted to be calm for you and your daddy, but I'm not doing a very good job of it."

Ever since we'd found out we were pregnant, I'd tried to keep a positive attitude. It had taken so long for us to conceive that I'd wondered if it would ever happen. When I got that positive test, I'd worried about having another miscarriage, but things had progressed so beautifully that it had felt more like a dream. Then I'd turned into a grouch at the beginning of the third trimester, and about six weeks ago, Maverick had started freaking out about everything, constantly worried about me and the baby.

I got it. He was scared of something happening to one or both of us. I secretly thought it was adorable, even though I acted annoyed by his overwhelming overprotectiveness. I thought if I was the calm one, then Maverick wouldn't have any reason to stress. But suddenly, I wasn't calm at all.

At the hospital, Mila pulled up to the women's center and jumped out. After running inside, she returned a moment later with a man who was pushing a wheelchair. He was at least thirty, with arms bigger than even my husband's. Opening the passenger door, he gave me a grin as he lifted me effortlessly and placed me in the wheelchair.

"The fuck you doing, picking up my wife?" Maverick's deep voice boomed as he and his dad walked quickly toward us.

"Mav!" I cried, pulling his attention to me. There was murder in his eyes until they landed on me. "I'm in labor."

He bent to kiss me. "It's okay, baby. Don't worry. Everything is going to be okay."

Seeing how calm he was eased a little more of my panic. "Promise?"

"I promise, baby." He kissed me again before rubbing his hand lovingly over my stomach and straightening. To the male nurse, he growled, "I'll push my wife. Just show us the way."

It took less than twenty minutes to get me into a room, examined, and for the doctor on call to have the team of nurses prep me for the C-section. By then, Mav's mom and my parents had arrived.

"What's taking so long?" Dad grumbled as he paced the width of my private room. He kept combing his fingers through his hair, disheveling it more and more, giving him an almost deranged look with his face so pale. "She's in labor. They should be doing something."

"They are," Mom hissed at him. "We're just waiting for them to come get her. You need to relax, because you're freaking our little girl out right now."

He blanched then walked over to my hospital bed where I was already hooked up to monitors and an IV. "Sorry, sweetheart. I'm just..."

"I'm sorry we won't be able to have our date tomorrow night," I told him in hopes of distracting us both. "I was really looking forward to dinner together."

"Me too, sweetheart."

I reached for his hand, and he readily took mine, holding on to it tightly. His was sweaty with nerves, and my heart melted. In the past three years, our relationship had come a long way. It had been slow to start, just a father-daughter date every couple weeks to begin with because I'd still been so angry with him. But he'd worked hard to earn back my trust and heal the broken pieces of my heart.

"I'm disappointed because I won't be able to tell you that Mav and I decided on Rocco's middle name." I looked up at my husband, who winked down at me. "We thought Rocco Colton-James Masterson sounded too good together not to give it to our son."

Dad sucked in a sharp breath at the same time Uncle Spider did too.

"You..." Dad paused to clear his throat. "You're naming him after both of us?"

"Well, he already acts like both of you," I said with a small laugh. "I figured it was only fitting to give him both of his grandpas' names."

"River, I don't know what to say," he said in a choked voice. "I—"

The door opened, and the doctor came in with two nurses. "Are we ready to have a baby?" he asked as the nurses started unhooking the machines I was plugged into that monitored Rocco.

"Definitely," Maverick told the man. "The sooner, the better."

My panic began to take over again. Seeing it, Dad bent and kissed the top of my head. "You're going to be fine, little girl. Maverick won't let anything happen to you. Be brave," he whispered. "We'll all see you soon. Okay?"

I nodded, fighting tears.

"Love you, River."

"I love you too, Daddy."

Hours later, after everyone had gone home for the night, I sat up in bed with Maverick beside me helping me hold our son for the first time. I was in some major pain, but the medication made me not care. Maverick was helping me hold Rocco because I was all kinds of loopy, and I didn't want to risk dropping my precious baby boy.

"He's beautiful," Mav whispered. That was how he'd been talking since Rocco had been placed in his arms earlier. As if he were afraid to raise his voice any louder for fear of scaring our son.

But he didn't need to worry. Rocco was already fearless. Other than crying when he was first pulled from my tummy, he'd been calm and wide-eyed. Mom had joked that he was taking the world in and finding it all rather boring, but I thought she was pretty spot-on.

"He looks just like you," I told him as I traced my finger down Rocco's cheek. The baby made a humming sound deep in his throat, and I couldn't help falling a little more in love with my son.

"Nah, I see a little of you in him too, babe. See this nose?" He was still whispering. "That's your nose. And those eyes? I think they're going to be green and not gray like mine. And this chin? I would know this chin anywhere."

"Yeah?" I asked hopefully.

He touched his lips to the tip of my nose. "Yeah, baby."

I rested my head on his shoulder and turned my gaze back on our little miracle. We sat there quietly, taking in Rocco's perfection for the longest time. When something wet dripped down my face, I rushed to wipe it away and realized I was crying.

"Baby, what's wrong?" Maverick asked in a pained voice, but still whispering.

I laughed a little and scrubbed at my cheeks. "I'm just so happy."

He groaned and pressed his lips to my forehead. "Me too, River. Me too."

Turn the page for a sneak peek at the next book in the
Angel's Halo MC Next Gen Series, *Her Shelter*,
featuring Max and Delaney.

HER SHELTER

ANGELS HALO MC NEXT GEN BOOK 6

The beautiful, ethereal creature ran across the road on my way home one night. I nearly hit her and ended up wiping out in the process. A little dazed, I ran after her...

And found her in the woods. Dirty and cold from living on the streets for weeks—but still so breathtaking, I was sure I was dreaming her.

Delaney is deaf, scared, and on the run from her uncle.

But now that I've found her, I won't let anything hurt her ever again.

She makes me feel something I've never felt before. This tightness in my chest causes the beast within me to snarl unless she's beside me. She becomes my obsession, my reason to get out of bed in the morning. She makes me want to be...better. For her.

I'm never letting this girl go.

No matter who tries to take her from me.

HER SHELTER PROLOGUE

DELANEY

Hunger twisted in my stomach, gnawing on my insides, making it hard to focus on anything but the empty feeling. I couldn't remember the last thing I'd eaten, and even then, it had been a small serving from the soup kitchen in Oakland.

I hadn't gotten to finish it because I'd thought I saw one of Uncle Tony's men outside the shelter, and I knew I couldn't chance being found.

My uncle wasn't a good person. There was a reason my parents had never talked about my dad's sister and her husband. But when they died, I had no choice but to go live with them. When the social worker dropped me off, sticking around to make sure I settled in, Aunt June and Uncle Tony had been so nice and welcoming.

The moment she left, however, things had changed drastically.

I shuddered, not just from the chilly spring night air on my bare arms, but from the memories of having spent the last eight years under the same roof with those two evil monsters. I was ten when my parents died. We'd been on vacation in Belize when a gas line had exploded.

Our hotel was right on the water, only a quarter of a mile from the gas line. Dad and Mom were standing on the balcony of our hotel room enjoying cups of coffee when the explosion happened. I'd just walked out onto the balcony, already begging them to take me down to the beach.

Dad saw what happened and jumped up, scaring me more than the sudden loud noise. There wasn't time to react, but he'd tried so hard. He pushed Mom and me into the hotel room, using his own body to protect us from the blast.

I was knocked unconscious from the force of the blast and didn't wake up for nearly a week. When I opened my eyes, it was to discover I was not only an orphan, but also completely deaf.

By the time Aunt June was tracked down and I arrived at her house, I knew some sign language to help me communicate, but I mostly got by with reading lips. My aunt and uncle treated me like I was an idiot, and I was placed in a school for the disabled. Most of the kids in my classes were just as deaf as I was, but the majority of them had been born not being able to hear.

The silence I was suddenly enveloped in every moment of the day made me feel alone in the world, even when I was surrounded by people. Aunt June and her husband didn't even attempt to learn sign language to try to communicate with me. When I wasn't at school, they kept me in my room. Their housekeeper brought me meals and washed my clothes, but other than that, I had no human contact with anyone if I wasn't at school.

Then, the day before my eighteenth birthday, Marta, the housekeeper, appeared in my room with a bag in one hand and fear in her eyes. She grabbed my face and spoke slowly, knowing I could read lips.

"You have to run, *mija*," she'd mouthed. "It's not safe for you here."

"Why?" I'd asked, confused.

"They are bad people." The urgency I'd felt vibrating off her only made me anxious. "Please, Delaney. You must go. You're not safe."

"But..." I'd started to argue, but she'd pushed the bag into my arms.

"I gave you some money and food. There are clothes and things you will need. Run, *mija*. Run, run, run. Please." She wrapped her arms around me, and I felt her tears on my neck. When she pulled back, her eyes were already swollen. "Run and don't ever let them catch you."

I didn't understand why she was making me run, but I knew she was right. Aunt June and Uncle Tony were evil people. From my bedroom window that overlooked the driveway, I'd seen some of the men who came and went. I'd also seen the women they brought with them.

I ran, and I kept running. From one town to the next, keeping my head down, living in shelters and eating at soup kitchens when my money ran out. Something that happened all too quickly because Marta hadn't given me much cash. In my heart, I knew she'd given me what she could, but it hadn't been enough to last even a week.

From Oakland, I'd hitchhiked north. The trucker who'd dropped me off the day before had stopped in some little town called Creswell Springs, and while he'd been in the gas station just off the interstate, I'd made a run for it. The guy had given me a bad feeling, and after having been on the streets for the past two months, I'd learned quickly to listen to that particular feeling.

That was two days ago, and I'd been sleeping in the woods during the day and exploring the small, quaint little town at night. There wasn't much to it, but it seemed safe enough.

My stomach clenched painfully as I walked past a building with a sign that read Ink Shoppe on the window. The lights were off, but a motorcycle and a small white car were in the back parking lot. I'd noticed there were a lot of motorcycles in Creswell Springs. Every man who rode one had a cut that said Angel's Halo MC on the back, but for some reason, they didn't scare me. Not like the men in suits who came to Uncle Tony's house did.

As I rounded the corner of the Ink Shoppe, the back door opened, and I quickly stepped into the shadows. A tall guy with short, dark brown hair stepped outside and opened one of the trash cans. After depositing the bag in his hands, he placed the lid back on it and walked back inside.

I'd seen the outline of a pizza box in that trash bag, and tears filled my eyes as my stomach cramped yet again.

No, I told myself as I turned to walk away. That was gross. Eating food that had been put in the trash was disgusting. I couldn't. I wouldn't.

I walked farther down the road, sticking to the shadows so no one could see me. But no matter how hard I tried to think about anything else, all I could see was the trash bag and the possible pizza box inside. Was there any left? Could there be a piece still, or even some crust? Were there other things in that bag I might be able to eat?

I just needed a little food. Something, anything, to make the pain in my stomach go away.

Pressing a fist to my mouth, I bit down on my knuckle, hoping the pain in my flesh would distract me from the crazy thoughts in my head—and the pain inside me.

An hour passed, and suddenly I was running back to the Ink Shoppe. The discomfort was just too much to take anymore. I was starting to feel dizzy, and I knew if I didn't eat something soon, I was going to be too weak and sick.

When I reached the shop, the motorcycle and the car were still in the parking lot, but all the lights were off inside. The smell of the trash from the other can was rancid, but that didn't stop me from tearing the lid off the one I'd seen the guy open earlier.

In my rush to get to what was inside, the trash can tipped over, crashing to the ground at my feet. Scared, I looked around frantically, unsure how loud the noise had been, but I'd felt a small vibration in my feet, so I knew there had to have been enough ruckus to alert someone to my presence.

Shaking from hunger and fear of being discovered, I quickly tore open the trash bag and pulled out the pizza box. There was also a foil container that smelled like it might have held pasta, and I grabbed that as well. Holding on to them like a lifeline, I took off at a dead run back into the woods.

When I was a good distance away, making sure the shop was out of sight, I stopped and fell to my knees, unable to go another inch because I no longer had the energy.

My sobs made my chest vibrate as I opened the pizza box in the dark and felt around inside for something to eat.

When my fingers touched a small piece of crust, I closed my eyes and stuffed it into my mouth, trying not to think about the fact that I was eating trash. As I chewed, I felt for more, hoping there would be something else. There was half a piece, and from the feel of it, half the toppings were missing. It was basically just bread and a little sauce, but it tasted so good, it brought tears to my eyes.

Dropping onto my bottom, I pulled the box onto my lap, but it was empty now. Placing it on the ground beside me, I reached for the foil container. With the trees blocking out all light, I couldn't see what, if anything, was inside, so I just stuck my hand into it. The spaghetti felt slimy, but when I lifted a handful to my mouth, it tasted good.

As with the pizza box, there wasn't much inside, but it was enough to make the pain in my stomach ease a little. But as I swallowed the last bite, I felt sick.

I'd just eaten trash.

Disgusted with myself, I pulled my knees up to my chest and pressed my forehead to my thighs as I willed the contents in my stomach to remain there. After a few minutes, the sick feeling eased, but I stayed where I was.

The loneliness I'd felt since waking up to complete silence all those years ago pressed down on me, making my heart ache. I missed my mom and dad. I even missed Marta. She didn't have a lot of contact with me, but she'd been the only one to care for me over the past eight years.

Now, I was homeless and starving. There was no one to care if I was hungry or warm or safe.

There was only me, and I was doing a craptastic job of taking care of myself.

I sat there and cried until there were no tears left, but that could have just as easily been because I was dehydrated.

Forcing myself to stand, I brushed the dirt off my clothes and walked farther into the woods to find somewhere to sleep for the night.

COMING **2.25.2021**

PLAYLIST

"My Oasis" ft. Burna Boy by Sam Smith
"Let's Love" by David Guetta & Sia
"We Belong" by Dove Cameron
"Mess Me Up" by Neon Tress
"I See Red" by Everybody Loves an Outlaw
"Killing Me Slowly" by Bad Wolves
"Him & I" by G-Eazy & Halsey
"Tell Me You Love Me" by Demi Lovato
"My Heart's to Blame" by Falling in Reverse
"Human" by Christina Perri
"Your Guardian Angel" by The Red Jumpsuit Apparatus
"Wonder" by Shawn Mendes